ENDORSEMENTS

"Life After E.L.E. left me dumbstruck . . . and happy and sad and excited and weepy and a little bit in love. It's very Hunger Games meets The Day After Tomorrow. If you are looking for an exciting fast-paced read, this is the story for you!"

~ **Julie Hall,** USA Today Bestselling Author

"An extremely well written book with a consistent, almost breathless pace. You will find yourself completely immersed in this. Move over Hunger Games, a new challenger has arrived on the scene!"

~Readers Favorite, 5 stars

"The author writes an action packed story that will keep you on the edge of your seat trying to read faster and turn the pages faster to see what is going to happen next."

~ Goodreads

"Full of action, suspense and a world turned cold!"

~ Goodreads

"This is a true dystopian fantasy novel, but it has its own uniqueness rather than riding the coat tails of previous works, as so many seem to do."

~Missica Skeens Pullen

"Engaging and full of suspense, JC's work keeps me on the edge of my seat ... from the first paragraph, I found myself unable to put down the story until the very last word."

~ **Naomi Miller** , author of the ***Amish Sweet Shop Mystery*** series

"Life After E.L.E. provided all the elements to keep me interested throughout December. My evenings were filled with action, suspense, and romance."

~ Jannette Fuller

Escape after E.L.E.

BOOKS BY JC MORROWS

Order of the MoonStone series

A Reluctant Assassin

A Treacherous Decision

A Desperate Escape

A Tragic Consequence

A Broken Kingdom

Frozen World series

LIFE AFTER E.L.E.

ESCAPE AFTER E.L.E.

LIBERTY AFTER E.L.E.

(COMING SOON)

WITH MACY MORROWS

Tales of a Teenage Alien Human Hybrid

THE ALIEN'S DAUGHTER

(COMING SOON)

Escape after E.L.E.

FROZEN WORLD - PART TWO

JC MORROWS

Mystic Moonstone Press, Knoxville, TN
www.mysticmoonstonepress.wordpress.com

ISBN: 978- 0998169231 (Trade Paperback)
ISBN: 978-1948733434 (Hardbound)
ASIN: BO79V1M9B9 (Kindle)

1. Teen Fiction / Post-Apocalyptic. 2. Teen Fiction / Dystopian. 3. Teen Fiction / Action & Adventure / Survival Stories. 4. Teen Fiction / Clean Read.

This novel is a work of fiction. Names, characters, places and incidents are either products of the author's imagination or used fictitiously. Any similarities to real persons, locations or events are purely coincidental.

Hardbound Edition 2023

For everyone who got me
through that first
NaNoWriMo!

PROLOGUE

Arizona Caves

Year 45 A.E.

Day 171

The muscles in my arms were straining as I struggled against the guards who held me in place. I shouted, but who could have heard me over the tremendous sound of metal on metal as the gates closed between Eve and the group of us struggling to break free of the guards. . .

Beside me, I heard a grunt and then Sierra was rushing for the rapidly shrinking gap between the gates. She nearly made it before three guards knocked her off her feet and dragged her back.

I tried calling out to Eve, to tell her to run faster, but my words came out in a croak. One of the guards must have hit me harder than I'd realized.

Please God, let her make it. Please?

When Eve stopped, looked up at the wall beside us, snapped a jaunty little salute, and then ran back toward the forest, my heart felt as if it stopped. . . went cold. . . drained of every ounce of life. And though I still struggled with the guard that held me, my heart was no longer in it.

My heart was on the other side of the gate; with the woman I could never have expected to fall in love with.

Every step she took away from me felt like a knife sinking deeper into my chest—the pain like a floe of ice rushing through my veins. . . . until I caught sight of Eve one more time. Through the now-tiny gap between the gates, I saw her enter the forest.

She was moving fast now, likely trying to find some sort of shelter for the night—and I tried to hold on to that, find some comfort in it. She would do whatever she must to survive. I knew that. Eve was a fighter. A survivor. She would find a way. I felt it as certainly as I felt the cold filling my chest.

But when the gap disappeared, when the gates were closed,

when the guards released their hold on me, that hope evaporated with the final dull, hollow, clang—and I dropped to my knees on the hard, cold ground.

It was no more than a second until I felt other hands holding onto me, lifting me off the ground, pulling me from my hopeless pose.

"Jude, she's smart."

"She'll find a way. I know it."

"Don't give up on her."

I heard the words. They sank into my thoughts, but there was no hope in them. There was no hope for Eve's survival. If there was anyone who could have survived outside the gates, my father would have been the one. And he had not—even though he had been prepared for it.

So how could there be any hope for Eve?

"Come on, Jude. This isn't helping her."

"Yeah, man."

"We need to get you inside, get you some rest."

"We'll go out first thing in the morning to look for her. She's smart. She'll make it."

The hands were pulling at me again, tugging me along with them.

I turned. . . followed. . . but all I felt was cold.

Not again, Lord. Please not again. I don't think I can survive it this time, Lord God. Help me. I cannot handle losing her.

PART 1

JUDE

ONE

Arizona Caves

Year 45 A.E.

Day 173

The forest around me was especially dark, even though I knew it was only midday.

There must be a storm coming.

I continued to follow the tracks I'd found, tracks much too small to have been made by a man's foot, tracks which moved in the precise direction I was certain they would have. Each impression made it clear she had been running quickly, nearly flying over the ground—and I was thankful there had been no fresh snow during the night to cover or fill them in.

It is good news for her. The weather last night was favorable.

That is certainly to her benefit.

And I hope that was enough. There was an itch between my shoulder blades as I followed the tracks even more deeply into the forest. I ignored it, focusing completely on the impressions in the snow I hoped would lead me to her, speeding up as the ground smoothed out and the trees spread farther apart.

And then I stopped.

The tracks in front of me now were worrisome, but not nearly as troubling as the deep red stain in the snow beside them. Looking over the deep depressions in the snow, the wide swath of snow swept from one side to the other, the smashed prints, the deep indentations where something sharp had pierced the snow. . . and that telltale sign of blood, I could picture the scene unfolding in front of me as if I were watching it happen.

Clearly someone had been attacked here.

Looking at the evidence that indicated a struggle, I moved around the scene, trying to determine which direction the animal had run off in—and what had become of their prey.

It took only a moment to discover both. To a ninety degree angle, there was the unmistakable path of something. . . *or someone*. . . being dragged.

And somehow. . . I knew it had not been the animal.

I changed course, readying my knife and short sword. The

crossbow would have to wait until I had the beast in my sights.

If it has hurt her. . . I cut the thought off as bile rose in my throat.

I continued to track the beast, following along the side of the deep path in the snow, panic clutching at me with the lack of any signs that the prey had been struggling.

What if this was another of those snowy tigers? Would she have had a chance against it by herself. . . taken by surprise. . . in a hurry. . . in the dark? Even though the answer felt frighteningly obvious, I forced the panic down, concentrating on finding her before I jumped to any more conclusions. That would certainly not help me now. I knew I needed focus, and caution, if I was going to find her.

My steps faltered when I saw that the blood trail—which had been thinning significantly the last few yards—stopped abruptly. I wanted to search the area for signs that the beast's victim had somehow managed to get away, but all I had to do was look ahead to see that the signs of something being dragged through the forest was still very much evident, so I continued to follow the tracks.

Several yards further, the trail changed direction—so I did as well. I could not help but notice that the tracks were significantly deeper here. . . had been for some time actually. It looked as if the victim had lost consciousness.

Or else. . .

Once again, I forced my thoughts away from such conclusions.

Stopping for a minute to take several deep breaths, I rolled my shoulders, attempting to release some of the tension that felt as if it had taken permanent residence there.

This is ridiculous. I need to stop making conclusions about what I think might have happened. Until I find hard evidence, I can only continue to track the beast and its prey. Only once I find one or the other, can I truly come to any solid conclusions.

My mind settled again as I stepped forward—pushing through a clump of underbrush—and all thoughts of calm or focus left me.

There. . . lying in the snow. . . covered in blood and pale as the death that had clearly taken her from me. . . was the only woman I had ever truly loved.

I sat up with a start, my shout echoing all around the tiny room, the sound of my thundering heart nearly deafening in my ears.

Light from the hallway spilled into my room as the hatch opened and my aunt rushed in.

"What is it, Jude! What's wrong?"

I dragged a hand across my face, wiping away sweat and moisture as I did. I sat there; tangled in the thick coverings, each breath a struggle, as I attempted to make sense of the scenes still vividly flashing through my mind.

"I do not know. A dream perhaps. . ."

"Eve?" Her voice was soft, but I heard the name clearly enough—and felt the all-too-familiar pain in my chest at the thought of what had become of her.

I could only nod in return. A glance at the digital on the wall of our common hallway reminded me that it had not yet been even two full days since the gates had shut her out of the city, though it felt as if it had been an eternity.

Two A.M.—what is it about that time of morning? There was a vague memory that told me it was a significant time, but the images of a certain mangled and bloodied body lying still and lifeless in the snow refused to give way.

"It has been two days, *machaon.* Do you not think you should try to find some way. . ." She stopped speaking when I pushed away and scrambled from the bed.

"I will not give up on her." I moved quickly to the hall before she could say anything further.

My bare feet made almost no sound on the smooth metal floor as I made my way to the small bath we shared with two other compartments in the section—though the sweat that had yet to dry on my chest had already succeeded in cooling the temper that had begun to churn within me.

I was thankful to find the area empty—even though there were several cubicles within. I wished for privacy, yet it was unusual, even in the middle of the night, to find no one else inside. For once, I was thankful for the chill of the water that rushed from the tap. It was several seconds before it began to slow. . . and heat up a little, but by then I was ready to turn it off. Between the dried sweat and the fever that had burned inside and out since the gates had closed between us. . . it was tempting to slip under the cold spray of the shower, but the sound of footsteps outside likely meant Aunt Galyna had come to check on me.

Determined to keep calm, I shook excess water from my face and hair, drying only my hands before making my way back into the hall.

"I meant no disrespect, Jude. I understand it is hard for you. I only wish to help."

It took only a moment for guilt to make itself known. "I know, *Titka,* please forgive me. I suppose the dream rattled me more than I knew."

Sweat and water forgotten, I leaned down to wrap my arms around my diminutive aunt. We might be surrounded by our own, but the connection to our neighbors was tenuous at best. She was the only family I had left and the same was true for her. I could never let myself forget that.

But losing Eve had made me even more aware of that fact.

"I worry for you, *machaon.* It is too much that you must go through this again." Her slim arms tightened at the reminder. . . a reminder I was surprised to realize was lacking the hurt it would have caused only a few months before.

"It is different this time, *Titka.* Eve is. . ." The words escaped me at the sudden overwhelming realization that by now I should likely be referring to her in the past tense.

Even if she could have survived that first night. . . I could not bear to finish the thought. Fierce storms had raged again and again since the gates had closed between us—almost as if the elements themselves were out to get her. Even if she had found shelter, it was becoming less and less likely that we would find her out there. . . still alive.

TWO

Arizona Caves

Year 45 A.E.

Day 174

Metal collided with metal as Adam dropped his tray onto the table beside me—and the sudden noise shook me out of my thoughts. I looked up at the man who had nearly become my shadow the past two days. It did not take much to see that whatever news he had was not good.

"These people. . . I swear. It's like they just don't care. It's like Eve, Malcolm and the others are not important at all."

There was no surprise in his voice, just resignation; a feeling that had been fighting to find a home in my own heart as well.

It was a struggle to keep a tight reign on the temper that had been boiling beneath the surface since those gates had begun to close—and the guards had kept me from going after her, but that same temper was the only thing that kept me from sinking into despair.

Especially once we discovered Malcolm was also missing. It had taken a full day to get confirmation, and by then, we had all been ready to storm the gates.

"Hey, did you know Eve's grandfather is a guard?"

Adam's question took me by surprise, but I answered immediately, absently, "Yeah. I did."

I stopped then, thinking about what else I knew of Eve's family. Sadly, there was not much. I knew only about her grandfather because of her explanation about what had happened to her father. We had been together such a short time—and we had not discussed much in the way of our families.

We really did not talk much at all. A heated memory quickly came to mind; frantic kisses, hands pulling each other closer, the fear of discovery lending a sense of the forbidden. It sent an unexpected shaft of pain into my chest.

If only we had known how little time we had left. I pushed the thought away, suppressing the anger that threatened to consume me. Time was precisely the reason we had not felt any need to discuss family. We had focused only on each other, well aware that—whether in the caves or out there in the forest—any given day could end with one or both of our deaths.

The clatter of another tray pulled me from my thoughts again. Across from me, Sophia was settling onto the bench, her movements heavy and stiff. She had become even more sullen in the last few days. If that were possible.

I could not be sure if it was because of Eve or the loss of Jordan. I would not have thought she and Eve were close. . . but perhaps it was just one more thing she and I had never spoken of. "Is there any news? Any good news?" The defiance in her voice gave me some hope. She might not be able to force anyone to let her out—none of us had managed that as yet—but she had clearly not given up on Eve either. Or perhaps she just wanted out of the caves as much as I did.

"No, no good news."

I looked up sharply at the oath she uttered, loud enough to draw sharp looks from the people at neighboring tables. "Oh, shut up!" She purposely spoke loud enough for those sitting at the nearby tables to hear, but did not direct her comment at anyone in particular.

"You don't have to be like that, Sophia." I tried not to notice the looks our table was getting. One thing we didn't need was to call attention to ourselves. Nothing good would come of it.

I looked over as Lily slid onto the bench beside me. She said nothing, but gave my shoulder a squeeze as she settled herself on the seat. Across from us, Sophia grumbled something and then stood, taking her still-full tray with her as she stormed away from the table.

"She just needs time." Lily's quiet voice should have been soothing, but there was too much of the same anger and frustration within me that Sophia had no trouble spewing over anyone within arms reach.

"No, Lily. I know just how she feels. We are out of time." Adam's voice was quiet, but fierce—which was oddly comforting. "Something has to be done. Now."

At least I am not alone in my frustration and anger.

"Yes, but what can we do? We're just a bunch of kids. I'm not certain we even officially graduated that stupid class."

"Are you really worried about class right now?" Adam's voice was harsh, angry, as he nearly snarled at Lily.

"No, Adam, I'm not worried about class. I'm wondering how we are supposed to get anyone to let us out if we didn't finish the class."

A weight settled in my stomach at her words. *What if Lily is right. With Eve not making it back in and us fighting with the guards, will they even let us out to search for her?*

I looked up when Jake dropped his tray across from mine on

the table, in front of the seat Sophia had just vacated. His expression was grim, his movements showing the frustration we all felt.

“Something wrong, Jake?” Lily spoke tentatively, then waited with the rest of us for an answer.

“I've been called to report to botany in the morning.” Next to me Lily let go the breath she had clearly been holding while Adam reached across the table and smacked Jake on the shoulder. “Don't scare us like that, man.”

“Scare you. . . Does no one else remember what happened to Anna when she reported to her duty station?” A sound like a grunt came from Adam's throat as Lily gasped, but nether of them said a word. Likewise, I tried to think of something—anything—that I could say, but nothing came to mind.

We sat there for what felt like an eternity in silence before the sound of another tray sliding against the metal table provided a distraction.

Sierra slid onto the seat beside Lily, her expression one of hopelessness. I started to ask her if she had news, but something about her expression told me her feelings had nothing to do with Eve. I watched as Lily put an arm around Sierra's thin shoulders.

“How are you doing?” A shake of her head was the only answer Sierra gave.

As she sat there, quiet and withdrawn, I realized that it was almost as if she and her cousin had switched personalities. Sierra had been the one willing to face down anyone, frightened of no one, tough and angry, while Sophia had been the quiet one who kept to herself. . . at least until Jordon's death. Now Sophia had become the one who was almost frighteningly fierce. Since being released from the infirmary, she spent nearly all of her time in the workout room, going from machine to machine, demanding more and more of herself. Her sparring partners rarely left the mat without bruises and her weapon practice rivaled even the best we had seen from Eve.

At mealtimes she mostly chose to sit alone at one of the few single tables that dotted the irregular edges of the dining room, staring down anyone who dared approach. . . save us. She still rarely spoke—and when she did her voice was cold, hard, angry. There was no question that she had been changed by her experience. And it was easy to understand why her cousin worried for her. Gone was the sweet girl who had easily blended into the background of every crowd. In her place was a woman with murder in her eyes and acid on her tongue.

"You just have to give her time, Sierra. She's been through a lot."

Evidently I was not the only one who had noticed the marked difference. Sierra opened her mouth to reply—her words spoken through clenched teeth. "We've all been through a lot.

What makes her special?"

While I knew precisely how she felt, Lily's answer reminded me why Sophia had every right to withdraw into her own little world of misery—as I had been tempted to do more than once since the gates had closed between Eve and me.

"Come on, Sierra. She watched Jordan being beaten to death. I'd say she has a right to withdraw a little."

Sierra let out a shaky breath before answering. "It's just so hard to see her close herself off this way. I mean, she has always been a bit of a loner, but this is different. And as for the rest of it. . ." she shrugged, but said nothing else. We knew exactly what she was referring to.

Lily wrapped Sierra in a tight hug as tears began to slip down her pale cheeks. I looked down at the untouched food on my tray. It was difficult to see the toughest person in our class in such a state. Lily looked at me over Sierra's shoulder, but I had no more answers than anyone else. There was nothing any of us could do.

If she can't hold it together, what hope is there for the rest of us? My thoughts were interrupted by a deep voice, one I easily recognized.

"You guys up for a little field trip?"

Adam's knee bumped mine as we both turned to look up at our class instructor.

Surprisingly, it was Sierra who answered. "Absolutely." I turned to look at her in surprise. Her expression was more fierce than any I had ever seen her wear.

"Grab your gear and meet me at the gates in twenty." With that, he strode off, leaving us all scrambling to follow. . . all except for Jake. I watched him as he continued to sit there at the now empty table. His shoulders were stiff and he was picking at the food left on his tray. I tried to think of something to say, but everything sounded wrong as I went over it in my mind. I stood there for as long as I dared, trying to find some way to tell Jake that he would be missed. . . without it sounding like I was writing him off—when he looked up at me.

He said nothing—and neither did I, but after a moment he nodded, and I could see that he was not giving up. He was just accepting what was to be. He stood and squared his shoulders before walking away with his tray.

I turned to catch up with the class, stuffing as much of my uneaten food as I could into one of the bags stowed by the trash bins for just such a purpose. Then I snatched several go packs after dropping my nearly empty tray in the disposal box.

We would need the sustenance if we were going to be searching for hours.

"So, do you think this means he believes Eve is still alive?" Sierra's words were barely a whisper by my ear. "What else." I answered quickly, determined to save my breath. None of us were running. We knew that would draw too much attention, but every one was moving quickly. We all wanted to be the first one to the gate.

The master-at-arms met us at the equipment room door, passing out weapons quickly as we moved past her. She said nothing, as usual, but when she passed the crossbow into my hands, I thought I felt a bit of extra pressure against my hand before she let go. I looked up at her face, but she was already looking behind me at Adam.

There's no time now. I kept moving, going through the doorway, rushing to my personal locker, opening it as quickly as the system would allow and removing my gear, turning back to the doorway before the door had closed completely, shrugging into my coat as I went.

Sierra was the only one ahead of me when I moved into the hallway.

There was a tightness in my chest that I did not expect as I stood before the slowly opening gates. It was impossible to determine whether it was due to my last experience with them or to the fear that had turned to ice in my gut, the fear that I would find a scene like that of the one in my nightmare, on the other side of the gates.

Somewhere. . . she was out there. . . somewhere. The only question that remained was the state we would find her in.

"The storms are going to make it impossible to find much of anything in the way of tracks, but I figure we all know better than anyone else the best places to look." He spoke quietly, huddled close to us. "It would help if we came back with a kill or two while we're at it."

He stepped back then, speaking louder. "Stay in pairs. After those storms, the beasties are going to be in a foul mood."

I nodded right along with everyone else, but my mind was already racing ahead, thinking back to the paths Eve had preferred, the trails she had often followed, the places she had used as a makeshift hunting blind. I already knew the only way we were bringing back a kill was if one stumbled across our path.

I had one goal and only one goal for this outing.

A moment later we were walking through the gates and heading for the forest. I watched Lily and Jake veer off in one direction, Sophia and Sierra in another and Alan was following the instructor. I said nothing, but secretly I was glad Adam was the one beside me. He would search well, though he did not have as much experience with tracking as I did. I knew that he would not spend much time talking to me. Instead, he would watch my back and let me focus on tracking. In fact, nearly an hour passed before he said a word.

"Hey, this is where we took down that weird tiger."

I nodded somewhat absently, thinking back to the day I had sat high in a tree with Eve, watching for another of those tigers. That had been the first time she and I were partnered up in the class. We had sat in the tree for nearly a half hour before she asked me about the beast and how I had known what it was. At the time I had been annoyed at the interruption, but it had taken almost no time at all for me to see that Eve was genuinely interested and not just using the conversation as a way to get my attention.

Like so many of the young girls our neighbors have introduced me to since. . . I remembered the surprise that I had felt when I stopped myself from responding with my typical dismissal and had given Eve a chance. Memories assaulted me as we continued on, walking familiar trails; places where Eve and I had lay in wait for prey, spots where we had embraced passionately. Thoughts of conversations and companionable silences haunted me.

And all the while, we searched for any sign of her.

"Hey, Jude, can I ask you something weird?"

Adam's voice pulled me from my thoughts—and while I was grateful for the momentary absence of pain, I was also oddly annoyed at the interruption.

As such, I said nothing, nodding when he looked back at me.

"Does it ever bother you. . . the way she came back. . . so late? I mean, that's not like her at all. Yeah, she could be intense about staying on a trail, but remember how she was that day we found the tiger? She was going nuts about how late it was. I think she would have gone off and left us all if the rest of the class hadn't helped and got us moving faster."

It was a surprise to hear Adam voicing the same thoughts that had been in my own mind since the beginning. And had he been wondering as long as I—or was it only the reminder of that particular day which had brought it to mind?

"Do you ever wonder about that?" He asked again, his voice heavy with the question.

"I have, yes." I nodded sharply before going on. "She was quite intense about the gates. To be honest, I am more than somewhat surprised that she chose to train for hunting in the first place. Especially after what happened to her father."

"What happened to her father?"

"He was late for the gates as well." I kept the answer simple, hoping that Adam would not press for details I could not give.

"Oh man, that sucks."

"Indeed." However, thinking of her explanation about her

father, one detail bothered me considerably. It explained why she panicked when we were delayed by the tiger. It explained why she had always pushed to be early to the gate. It explained why, even when we were inside the compound, she had cringed every time the gates closed.

Why would she have been so late? It makes no sense.

"You are right about her determination to be on time, or even early, to the gate. And I believe I know why. When her father was locked out, she witnessed the whole thing."

"What! Are you kidding?"

Shaking my head, I explained. "Well, you know her grandfather is a guard."

Adam nodded and I went on. "She was delivering dinner to him that evening." As I thought about it, there was a strange feeling in my gut, an odd niggling at the back of my mind. Something was most definitely off about the whole situation.

Did someone purposely delay Eve? I looked up in surprise, when Adam voiced the very same question a moment later.

"Is it possible, do you think, that someone maybe did it on purpose, kept her away from the gate, I mean?"

I stood there, unable to answer, but Adam went on. "Is that crazy? I mean, why would anyone do something like that?"

"No reason I can think of, but somehow I don't think it's crazy, my friend."

We stood there for what felt like an eternity, both thinking over the possibility—one that felt crazy to even consider. And then we were moving again, both more determined than ever to discover something. . . anything. . . that might give us some clue as to whether we truly were mad or not.

None of us saw Jake at dinner that evening, but that was not much of a surprise since we came in at sunset and it took time to deliver our kills to the kitchen and stow our gear.

I was not the only one looking for him when we made our way across the dining hall to what had more or less become *our* table.

"He's fine." Lily's voice came from behind me and I turned to her a bit awkwardly, since I was already halfway in my seat. "He has a security escort as well, so he should continue to be fine."

"How did you find out?" Lily always seemed to know things before the rest of us and while I was grateful to know, it was more than a bit odd given how difficult information about other sections was to come by.

"I know someone who works in the same section. They

happened to be walking by when we came in and I asked." Something in the way she looked away from me while answering. . . and how she was careful not to say "he" reminded me of Sophia and Jordan's behavior and I nearly smiled, but then I was reminded of Eve—and the smile vanished quickly, leaving me to mumble a rushed "thanks" before I turned away and dropped the rest of the way into my seat. To her credit, Lily said nothing as she moved over to one of the other seats, though when I looked up a few minutes later, she offered me a sad smile.

THREE

Arizona Caves

Year 45 A.E.

Day 175

The mood at our table was surprisingly grim the next morning. I had expected that knowing Jake was safe and well-protected would be enough to put my classmates in a better mood. . . even putting aside our failure to find anything new about Eve or Malcolm. . . especially since Lily had filled the rest of the class in during our late dinner, but every face at the table held a dark expression.

Even Lily was not her normal bubbly, hopeful self. She sat across from where I stood, shoulders slumped, no smile on her delicate features, eyes red—as if she had cried most of the morning.

No one even seemed to notice when I stepped up to the table. Only after I stood there for several tense seconds, looking around at everyone's obvious misery and trying to work out what I could had missed between dinner last night and now, did Adam look up and meet my searching gaze.

"You haven't heard, then?" His voice was flat, emotionless, inscrutable and—somehow all I could think of was that blasted dream from a few mornings ago. Terrified that he was about to tell me someone had found Eve. . . just as she had been in the dream, all I could manage was a slight shake of my head.

"They found Jake this morning. He and his security escort. . ." He trailed off, but the picture was clear enough in my mind already, so I nodded—and dropped into the empty seat beside my friend. The food on my tray, which had looked inviting only a few moments before, no longer looked appetizing. Even the memory of the near party atmosphere we had returned to, loaded down with the prey that had all but leaped into everyone's paths, was not enough to lift anyone's spirits.

How could it possibly compete with such joyless news?

Looking around the table, I was oddly comforted by the fact that everyone at the table displayed the same look of mourning that I knew my face held. We all should have been celebrating, enjoying our spoils, reveling in what the rest of the caves' inhabitants deemed a very successful outing, but the loss of yet another friend made that a virtual impossibility.

"Are we going out again, do you know?"

I looked up at the question, surprised to see that it was Sophia speaking—and equally shocked at the sound of her voice. She sounded almost frantic, as if our very lives depended on the answer.

It only took a moment for me to realize that she might very well be correct. Out in the wilds we stood a chance, armed and prepared for a possible attack. Inside the caves we were clearly not safe.

Even with a security escort. The thought was no comfort.

"I don't see why not, given how much fresh meat we brought in." Adam spoke up beside me. "I mean, I think they'd be nuts not to let us have another go, right?"

I nodded, but said nothing.

Granted, when looking at our outing from my goals, it had not been at all successful. We had searched for hours, with no hint of a trail for either Eve or Malcolm. And while Lily had made the comment on our way back to the caves the day before that it was somewhat hopeful not to have found any remains, we all knew that was not really evidence that either of our friends had survived. However, Adam had the right idea. As far as the kitchens were concerned, we had been very successful. They would be crazy not to let us go back out again.

We sat in a companionable silence for the remainder of the meal. No one spoke. And no one left when the bell rang out, calling everyone to work. It was with more than a little reluctance that I stood, picking up the tray that was not quite empty. Adam called out to me a moment later.

"If you're not going to eat that. . ." He asked the question in a low voice, stopping when I held out my tray to him—and then exchanged it with his empty one, grateful that no one would give me grief for wasting food. I sat back down to wait for Adam. The others were still there, reluctant to leave.

It was less than twenty minutes later, when we had taken no more than a few steps out of the dining hall, that our questions from earlier were answered. Our instructor was waiting for us, already wearing some of his outdoor gear.

"Ten minutes," was all he said before we rushed off as a group.

I had taken no more than three steps before the feel of a hand on my arm stopped my forward progress.

"You are Jude, the young man who was interested in my granddaughter." It was not a question—and it took no more than a look to know that the woman was related to Eve. . . not Natalya.

I could only nod in answer.

"I know so little about you. Eve had only begun to mention you—" Her voice broke and she stopped speaking. The small hand on my arm tightened a bit. And I found myself wanting to reach out to her, find some way to comfort this woman who so closely resembled the young woman who still haunted not only my dreams, but every waking moment as well.

"Her mother and I would like the opportunity to know you." She spoke softly, looking down at the floor instead of up at him.

"I would like that, as well." It was a surprise to realize that I meant every word.

"Tonight then, you will dine with us." Another statement.

"Yes. I will be there."

She said nothing else, only nodded in return. A moment later I turned at Adam's shout behind me. "I have to go now."

"Take great care." She spoke quietly—almost a whisper—so that I barely heard her words, before she turned and quickly walked away.

I watched for several long seconds before turning and jogging to catch up with Adam and everyone else.

Eve's grandmother was waiting in the great hall when our class emerged from stowing our gear. Immediately, I was struck with the thought of how closely she resembled her granddaughter. Everything, from the way she stood, to the expression in her deep brown eyes, reminded me of the girl I loved.

When I reached her, she nodded sharply without speaking, then turned and walked down the hallway. I followed closely, even though I knew exactly where Eve's quarters were.

She had mentioned earlier that Eve had only begun to talk about me so I was unsure how much they knew about my relationship with her. Did they know I had been with Eve the night we were attacked? Did they know that I had begun waiting for her each morning after that so that I could walk with her to class? Did they know just how many rules about couples that Eve and I had broken—from our age difference. . . to finding dark places in the hallways, just to be together? And had she told them just how close we had come to breaking the most important rule?

Somehow I doubted that. If Eve had told them, they would likely want nothing to do with me—much less want the chance to get to know me.

As we drew nearer to the place where Eve had grown up, I began to regret agreeing to dine with her family. *What was I thinking?*

Aside from all of the things they obviously did not know—about rules being broken or the specific danger our entire class had been in for reasons still unknown, the most likely reason they wanted this chance to meet with me must be our renewed hunting activities.

They must have guessed that we have been searching for her when we go out.

And having no news. . . nothing good. . . or even bad, would only hurt them. I knew it to be true because it was nearly killing me. And now I had committed myself to what was shaping up to be a very uncomfortable evening.

Walking through the hallways closer to their living quarters, memories assaulted me, of being in these very halls with Eve, holding hands and walking slowly to stretch out every minute of time we could find to be together, of tucking ourselves into dark corners and stealing kisses while hoping no one came along and discovered us.

As I followed her grandmother along the path that was already so familiar to me, I thought back to the few bits of information we had shared about our families. I knew her father had missed the gate years ago, so there would be no meeting him. Her grandfather was a guard. Her mother was a botanist. I had no idea about her grandmother and I could not remember if she had a brother or sister.

There was so much about each other we had never had time to learn.

"Did you know Malcolm well?" The question shook me out of my thoughts and reminded me that he had lived somewhere near Eve.

"No, sadly, I did not."

"He and Eve played together as children, but they lost touch for some time. Until they both signed up to train as hunters. . ." She trailed off there and neither of us said another word until we reached the door of their quarters.

"Before we go in. . ." she hesitated. I waited. We stood there for nearly a minute before she continued. "I just want you to know that, even though Eve only mentioned you a few times, I could see that she cared for you very much." She shrugged a little before adding, "A grandmother's eyes." Then she turned and I was left with the impact of her words.

So she did know. What did that mean for me? Did the whole family know? Had they been excited. . . waiting to welcome me into the family. . . or was her grandmother the only one who knew—and the rest of the family was only hoping I could give them some news about finding Eve?

Stepping across the threshold of Eve's quarters had less of an impact on me than looking into the haunted, tired eyes of her mother. Her resemblance to Eve was so unexpectedly strong, the icy fingers of pain that had gripped my heart since the gates had closed between us tightened painfully.

It helped very little to see that the woman before me had already given up on her daughter. She was grieving, but there was no trace of hope in her eyes or her body language. In her mind, Eve was gone and there was nothing to do now, but move on. The very idea of giving up sent another shaft of pain straight through me, but I did my best to tuck away those feelings. It was more than obvious they would not be welcome here.

"Thank you for joining us, Jude." There was an obvious strain in the woman's voice, and that immediately gave me pause.

Was this not her idea? But then . . . I did not need to finish the thought. It immediately became clear that Eve's grandmother was responsible for my invitation. I took a moment to think about what that could mean. Clearly she knew how Eve had felt about me. Was it possible that she had some idea how I felt about her granddaughter? And this dinner was because she felt cheated somehow?

Or was she really only thinking that I would be in the best position to find some way to rescue Eve? With that in mind, I bent slightly at the waist, hoping to convey respect, but to also acknowledge the kindness of her actions. "I am honored."

Eve's grandmother was the only one to return the gesture—before indicating the seat beside her at the table. I moved to stand behind the chair, but did not sit until both ladies had seated themselves.

Despite the atmosphere, which was strained and thick with tension, the meal was much better than anything I had ever eaten in the communal dining room. When I said as much, Eve's mother acknowledged my comments with a tiny voice, her words a barely understandable "thank you".

When the two women went on eating, I took the opportunity to study them more closely. There was as strong a resemblance between the two of them as there was between each one and Eve, though her grandmother held herself very differently than her daughter.

There was also a significant difference in their body language. It was more than just what she had already said to me today. There was something about the way Eve's grandmother moved that told me she shared my belief that Eve was alive out there somewhere.

Watching Eve's mother was a very different experience. There was nothing hopeful or determined in her posture or her body language. She was beyond grieving. She had completely given up all hope. . . and not just where her daughter was concerned.

Not that it's much of a surprise. She has lost her husband and now her daughter. It would be enough to drain anyone of all hope.

Before I could think any more about it, the main hatch opened and in walked the man who must be Eve's grandfather. He was dressed in the uniform of a guard, complete but for his empty weapon holster.

“Ah, this must be Jude, who we've not heard nearly enough about.”

Having stood when he entered the room, it was no trouble for him to look me over as he crossed the room. He did take me by surprise when he held out a hand to me. His grip was strong, vital, but without a trace of intimidation—though I could see that he was sizing me up the entire time.

FOUR

Arizona Caves

Year 45 A.E.

Day 176

I scrambled out of bed at the sound of the alarm on my bedside table, rubbing a hand over my face in an attempt to wipe away the fatigue. I swung my legs over the side of the bed and pushed my feet into my boots, thankful my morning routine took no real concentration at this point. Standing, I shook myself all over, attempting to start my blood pumping. I thought of the day ahead with a shiver. I would need to be alert—and another restless night was certainly not going to be helpful in that area.

Rubbing the sleep from my eyes, I tried to focus on our mission for the day. We had barely made it back through the gates the previous evening when someone from the kitchen staff had rushed over with a message from meteorology. Evidently they were expecting the temperatures to drop considerably in the coming days so the kitchen was counting on everyone to bring in a large catch.

Every hunting team was scheduled to go out and our instructor had already informed us that we would be going out extra early today.

Adam and I had talked it over as we stowed our gear—and we had both agreed that with the storms coming in, this would be our last chance to really look for signs of what had become of Eve. I'd been surprised that Adam felt as strongly about the whole situation as I did, given that I was the one so attached to Eve.

Considering the situation, the idea of going out and only bringing in kills that happened across our paths as we searched for Eve felt as if we were cheating the remainder of the class. Though Adam had been quick to tell me that everyone was counting on us to find Eve—or at least something that would answer the question of what had happened to her.

We needed some good news.

While I downed a quick-wake shake and then dressed as warmly as possible, I thought over the events from dinner with Eve's family. I had expected them to grill me about Eve and what we had found out about her thus far. I had expected them to have questions about our relationship. I had expected them to at least give me a token lecture about the dangers of flouting our rules about couples.

Instead I had been treated to a delicious meal, a few polite questions about myself, and told a few stories about Eve as a child. *All in all, a very confusing evening, one that left me with more questions than answers.* Especially with Eve's grandfather being a guard.

I pulled the rest of my clothing on in a hurry when I caught sight of the digital on my wall and rushed out into the hall. I had gone no more than ten steps before Adam fell into step with me.

"You're running late, Jude. Everything okay, man?"

"Everything is fine. I overslept—that's all."

"It's not like you to oversleep. You're always early." I could feel the intensity of his stare, worry-filled and focused.

"Not this early, though."

He was nodding before he answered. "Good point."

"Also, I have not been sleeping well. Nightmares." I lowered my voice on the last word, hoping he would drop the subject, but it was not to be.

"Eve?" The sympathy in his voice was obvious. However,

there was no tactful way I could think of to inform him that his curiosity was not helping, so I nodded tightly, again hoping that would be the end of it.

"I feel that, man. I can't even imagine how tough this is on you. I mean you two were so close." Fortunately we were in the main cave at that point and the noise level around us gave me the excuse to nod again as my answer. Looking around at all of the people rushing by us and heading in so many different directions, I was surprised to realize just how much I obviously missed on the average morning. . . getting a later start.

When we made our way past the crowd and stepped into the long line of other hunters waiting on the quick packs made up for our breakfast, and the go-packs we would take with us for later in the day—I brought the subject up to Adam, grateful there was much less noise here so that I could keep my voice low enough for only him to hear me.

"Can you believe all of this? How early must some of these people wake up every day?"

"I was just thinking the same thing. I never knew there were so many people awake and working this early." He was watching the crowd behind us, shaking his head a little as he said it.

"Do you know what amazes me? Some of them appear to be on the way to their job, but quite a few look as if they have already been working for some time."

"You know, you're right. Wow." He shook his head again before going on. "I mean, Wow. That is really something."

We moved through the line silently for several minutes, looking around us at the world we had never seen until today.

"Does it ever make you wonder. . ." Adam's voice trailed off before he finished his question, and when I turned to face him, he shook his head, saying quietly, "Later."

I nodded, understanding precisely what he meant. And I remembered hearing Eve say that there were things it was not safe to say inside the caves. When she had said it, I recalled feeling certain there would likely never be a time I might find myself in such a position. Yet, here I was; at a place where I must be exceedingly cautious of what I might say—and beyond that, what conversations I participated in. . . especially in light of what had happened to Jake. . . and Anna. . . and Jordan.

It was a somewhat daunting circumstance, standing in the midst of the caves, surrounded by people, the better part of an hour before we would be in the relative safety of the forest. But I was far more content to wait—than to take a chance with my own safety. . . or Adam's.

It was all the more surprising when—twenty minutes later, as we rushed away from the breakfast table—Eve's grandfather stopped me in the hallway. He appeared so suddenly, I did not even have a chance to speak, which was likely his intention because the first thing he did was to pull me into a dark corner.

Only when we were concealed in the darkness, did he speak, his voice so low it was difficult to hear.

"Don't speak. No questions. I cannot tell you how I know this, but you have been looking in the wrong place for her. I do not think she is where they think she is, but I have no proof. Only a gut feeling."

I started to speak then, but he shook his head and went on quickly. "If you think hard, you will know where to look. But you must be prepared. There may be no coming back if you go there." He stopped for only a moment—looking hard at me, before adding. "I believe she is still alive." And with that, he gave my shoulder a tight squeeze and was gone.

I stood there, thinking over what he had said for a full minute before moving cautiously out of the shadows and rushing to catch up with Adam.

When I bolted into the locker room, he looked up and opened his mouth to speak. I quickly shook my head, mouthing the word "later" before turning my attention to my gear and hopefully cutting off any chance of his saying something unfortunate here.

The hard, biting wind had me tucking the thick knit scarf tightly against the bottoms of my goggles before we'd gone more than ten feet from the gates.

"Hopefully it will calm down once we get into the trees." Adam was nearly shouting, yet I could barely make out his words. Together, we struggled against the wind with the rest of the class. Fortunately, he was right. The wind was blocked enough by the trees that walking became much easier as soon as we were surrounded by the towering evergreens and skeletal trunks of deciduous trees that would likely never leaf again.

We split into teams and took off almost immediately, each following our own different paths. Adam fell into step behind me and we set off. If he noticed the obviously different path I took, he said nothing about it. We walked for some time, clearly both aware of just how dangerous it might be if we were overheard—though I likely had a better idea now than I had before.

Too much of what Eve's grandfather had said reminded me of the doubts and fears Eve had shared with me. She and I had spoken only twice of our suspicions about how things really were in the caves, but both times I had gotten the impression that she knew more than she was telling me.

I understood her caution. Telling the wrong person anything you suspected about the caves or the Chancellor could be deadly.

Her grandfather must either have felt entirely certain I was trustworthy. . . or else he had been desperate—which, given the weather forecast and the time already passed, I understood completely. He had also been much too cautious for me to take his words or his message lightly. It was more than obvious that he was privy to information I could never hope to attain access to.

He knew something about Eve—and somehow that information told him she was more than likely still alive—and somewhere safe. . . and far away from the caves.

I didn't have to think hard to figure out where he meant she would have gone, but I did feel rather foolish for not considering the possibility earlier. Of course she would have headed to the city we had found. Even frozen over and devoid of life, it would have provided shelter and protection. Looking back at the circumstances and what I knew about Eve, I realized that should have been the first place I looked. She had likely been there all this time, waiting to be found—perhaps even afraid to return to the caves.

What else could explain her running away before she really even tried to reach the gates? Lost in my thoughts, I was only paying enough attention to the path we were taking and evidently Adam had finally decided we were safe enough to talk because he stopped suddenly and took hold of my arm when I kept moving.

"Okay, man. We're far enough away now that there shouldn't be anyone listening—so, the only chance is if someone is close enough to listen in—and I don't see anyone nearby. We should be safe for now." His words were all jumbled together, spoken so quickly that it was difficult to keep up. "What is going on?"

I took only enough time to gather my thoughts, knowing that Adam would be tempted to interrupt with questions—and I really wanted to get everything out. "Right. I had something very different I wanted to talk about, before Eve's grandfather stopped me."

Very quickly, I went over what he had said to me, holding up a hand when Adam started to interrupt. "I think you'll figure it out if you take a moment, but since time is of the essence. . ." With that, he closed his mouth and I went on quickly. "I think he was trying to tell me she went to that city we found by accident. I don't have a clue how he would know about the city. . . or how he knew that Eve knew about it, but it's the only thing that makes sense."

While Adam thought over what I had just said, I decided to throw everything else out there. . . let him deal with it all at once. "I have been thinking that there is some way they know we found the city. I don't have any idea what it could be, some sort of surveillance maybe, but they must know and obviously the Chancellor does not want anyone to know about it. I think that must explain what happened to Jordan, Anna and Jake."

"Wait." He broke in, his voice full of shock and disbelief. "You don't seriously. . ." He stopped just as suddenly as he had begun.

"I do. Think about it, Adam. We were getting a bit of negative attention over that tiger—not surprising when you think about it—but it was not until we found that blasted city that our classmates started being killed. Why would anyone do that over a little attention—especially since everyone would benefit from the meat. . . and the celebration?" I stopped then, giving him time to digest what I had said.

"Just what do you propose to do about it?" The question gave me hope. He might not believe everything had said, but he clearly didn't need to.

"This is where it gets tricky. Her grandfather said there might not be a way to come back. Think about that. We've been taught from the beginning that being out all night is a death sentence—and I think what he meant might just be that going to the city means we cannot return to the caves. If people figure out that the Chancellor is lying about that rule, they might begin to question everything. I do not believe he would allow that." I stopped again, waiting for the meaning behind my words to sink in.

Fortunately, it did not take long. "You mean, if we go there, we can't come back. . . ever?"

"I think that is precisely what it means, yes." When he said nothing, I added, "I am prepared to go alone. I am not asking you to come with me. I am merely telling you that I may not be returning. . . especially if I find Eve and she is safe."

"She means that much to you?" And that was all he said. There was already a look of acceptance in his eyes. He knew there would be no changing my mind so he was not going to try—and there were no words to explain just how much she meant to me. All I could do was nod.

"Then what are we waiting for?"

I started to move then. I took several steps before stopping, turning back. "Are you certain? You are prepared to leave everything. . . everyone. . . behind?"

He nodded first. Then, after a moment, he answered. "I have no one left there. . . no one." His voice broke a bit on the last word and, though I wanted to ask what he meant, I knew it was not the time so I turned and pushed on through the thick snow.

We walked for a long time in silence, listening to the forest around us for any signs of other people. With so many hunting teams out today, it was a very real possibility that we would cross paths with any one of them—and questions were the least of our concern. We had to make good time if we hoped to get through the forest, and out to the other side without being seen. Then we had to make it across the expanse of ice between the trees and the city, both without being seen by the other teams and without running afoul of a nasty predator. Being out in the open was never a good idea after a big storm and we both knew it.

Either out of boredom or from a desperation to keep me from asking probing questions, Adam spoke up after a time. "You know, you mentioned the guards. . . and I'm guessing the Chancellor. . . knowing stuff we don't know. How much of that do you suppose goes on right in front of us? How much happens in those caves that we don't see—that no one sees really?"

The questions brought me back to the times Eve and I had talked about the very same thing. Both of us had wondered about the very public execution everyone had witnessed just days before we had begun our hunting class. At the time, there had been no sense to the whole thing. So many young children and teenagers had been killed—with no trial, with no revelation of what their crime had been, with no explanations. And weeks had passed with nothing more being discovered. . . at least nothing that we knew or heard of.

"I am sad to say that I never gave the idea much thought. . .

until I met Eve, that is. You are right, Adam. There are most certainly things going on that we do not know about. And I believe that—at least in part—it is because some people do not really want to know."

"I hadn't thought of that. I mean, it makes sense, now that I think about it. With everything that goes on, being trapped in an icy cave, death being a very real possibility each and every day, who wants to think about how things really get done? Just as long as they're fed and sheltered, right?" His tone had become more angry with each word—and I found that I agreed with his anger.

If the people in the caves would only stand together, demand the truth, fight for freedom from the tyranny of a man who should not—if what my father had told me as a child was correct—even be our leader.

Almost immediately, I saw the flaw in those thoughts. In that same event that had ultimately caused me to begin wondering about all of this, the Chancellor had confirmed how foolhardy it would be to stand against him. He had guards everywhere in the caves. An uprising would only result in more groups pushed out into the swirling snow at two in the morning to freeze to death.

"I suppose they figure ignorance is safer. They turn a blind eye because they don't want to be the one in trouble." Clearly, Adam had already come to the same conclusion I had.

I nodded. "Eve and I talked about this very thing when we would hunt together. She, too, thought there must be things going on that we are not told about—dangerous things."

We walked in silence for several minutes before Adam spoke up again. "You don't think it's possible. . . I mean surely it's not. . . but I mean. . . " He stopped, turned to me and shook his head a little before speaking again.

"Do you ever think about what happened right before the gates closed on Eve that day, that little salute thing she did? And then she ran off into the forest? I mean, she didn't even really try to get to the gates, They didn't look that close to being closed when we first saw her. She might have made it. She was so close. But she just stopped, snapped a little salute and then turned away. You don't think. . ." He trailed off again at the last part of his question.

"I think about it a lot. At the time, I was only focused on her not making it back to the caves. I paid little attention to her actions—only the distance between her and the quickly decreasing space between the gates." I answered quickly, not really thinking about his question, but as I spoke I started to see the underlying question he was really asking.

I started to turn away, thinking that there was no possible way he could be right.

What possible reason would anyone have for wanting Eve dead? The thought had barely registered when I realized there was someone who would want Eve dead; whoever was responsible for Jordan's death, and Anna's death. They were most likely to blame for Malcolm's disappearance as well.

“This must be why Tim has us hunting in pairs or groups.” I was speaking mostly to myself, letting my thoughts wander as I did. “And it's probably why no one has put much stock in us finding a trace of Eve. . . or Malcolm. They don't want them to be found.”

“Yes, exactly.” Adam spoke forcefully. I looked over at him then, It was odd to think that he had been thinking of this all along. . . and keeping it to himself.

Turning away, I had only taken a few steps, when suddenly I felt a shiver run through my body. I looked around, searching for something. . . or someone. . . dangerous. “Adam—“

“Jude, run!”

PART TWO

EVE

FIVE

Hope City

Year 45 A.E.

Day I73

The person in front of me was moving slowly through the tunnel, holding his light just high enough for me to see the path ahead, but not enough that I could make out any distinguishing marks or what lay in the many openings we passed as we walked for what felt like miles.

If it was his intention to make me feel hopelessly lost, he had already achieved that goal. We could be walking in one continual circle for all I knew. . . and he could keep going forever and I would probably never know it. I wanted to speak up, to ask where we were—or where we were going, but something about the man's gruff demeanor told me I would get no answers from him.

Not that I expected answers from anyone.

"Here." He stopped suddenly, gesturing for me to walk through a doorway to his right.

I approached hesitantly. . . until I saw the light under the door. He swiped some sort of card against the wall beside the door too quickly for me to get a good look at it and the door opened with a little whooshing sound. He stepped back and I moved into the large room. A second later the door closed behind me.

I took a moment to let my eyes adjust to the brightly lit room after all the darkness and took advantage of the chance to look around the room as well.

I don't really know what I had been expecting after the dark, dank tunnel, but it certainly was not the warm, inviting room in front of me.

"Come in, miss."

I looked around for the source of the voice, surprised to hear such welcome—especially since everyone else I had encountered since waking up yesterday sounded like they couldn't wait to be rid of me. Or perhaps I had imagined it. . . and they were only doing their jobs. I had felt pretty rotten when I finally woke up. . . with a splitting headache and some pretty bad nausea to cope with.

It didn't take long to find the man standing by a small grouping of chairs and small tables. Curiosity got the better of me and I headed over to where he stood.

He gestured for me to sit and I sank down into one of the larger chairs, surprised at how comfortable it was.

He settled into one of the chairs across from me and turned his attention to the small device he held, the likes of which I had only seen once before, in the hands of the caves' mysterious master-at-arms.

I watched as he looked at the screen, trying to decide if I should ask a question or wait until he spoke to me. Fortunately, I didn't have to wait long. After less than a minute, he turned to me.

“Yes, well. What brings you to our little hidden city, Eve?”

My surprise cancelled out whatever I had meant to say first. “How do you know my name?”

He laughed before answering. “One of the first things we did was remove your personal tracker. It contains quite a bit of information about you.”

“When you say personal tracker. . .” I stopped and shook my head a little, trying to be certain I'd heard him right.

"Everyone in the caves is implanted with a personal tracker when they are about a year old. Initially it contains your name, your date of birth and information about your parents. As you grow and learn, more is added through data transmission."

My head was spinning with all this new information. Who in the caves knew that we had these things in our bodies? Why did we have them? *What possible reason. . .* But I already knew the answers to most of the questions racing through my mind. It was about control. The Chancellor wanted to know everything about everyone. . . all the time.

"So, you removed it to learn about me?" I carefully watched the man in front of me. Was I dealing with another Chancellor? Was the situation I had landed myself in any better than what I'd been dealing with in the caves?

"No. We removed it so that we would not give away our location."

"So, you didn't do it here?"

"No. We have a remote site where things like that are taken care of. I am afraid that is why Matteo knocked you out. You were much too close to the city. We had to get you to where it would be safe to remove the tracker before letting you into the city."

"He could have just said something."

He laughed before answering. "I presume he felt his actions were safest. We've all seen you shoot."

"You mean, you've been watching me?" I stopped there, trying to keep my cool.

"We watch everything that happens near the caves. It is as much for our own protection as it is for yours." He stopped there, but something about his tone and the abrupt stop made me think there was more to what he had said.

While I thought over his words, I realized I had a question about something he had said before. "You said my tracker contains information about me. Is it still active, then? You didn't destroy it?"

He shook his head before answering. "Destroying it would not be in the best interest of anyone here. It would give away the fact that someone found it, removed it, and destroyed it. We don't want anyone from the caves to know that you are here."

I nodded my head absently, but I was only half focusing on his answer. I was still thinking about everything he had said so far.

"Since Matteas found you just after sunset, my guess would be that you missed the gates. Am I correct?"

I started to speak, but stopped myself. If what he said was true and they watched everything that happened near the caves, he should know what had happened.

He waited for several seconds before his expression changed. "Ah, I can see that hunting is not the only area where you are quite proficient. You are trying to figure out just how much to tell me, how trustworthy I am, how likely it is that this is all some sort of trap." There was a flash of something in his expression, but it was gone too quickly to interpret before he added, "You catch on quickly," with a nod.

"All right. I will tell you what I know, then. I know you lost your father five years ago. I know that your grandfather is a guard and I know he was on duty when you missed the gates. What I don't know is why it appears as if you missed them, at least in part, on purpose."

I nodded to myself while he spoke, listening to his tone of voice and carefully watching his body language. By the time he had finished, I was certain that, while he might not be lying, he was holding something back. Certainly he knew more about me than the few drips of information he had mentioned so casually. He was fishing, trying to get me to trust him, tell him what he really wanted to know. What I needed to figure out was what he really wanted to know. . . and why. Why would the reason I had run away from the gates matter to him? Was there some chance this was all a trick? Was he feeding information to the Chancellor?

I had already seen firsthand that there were a myriad of places in the caves that I could never have imagined actually existing. It was perfectly reasonable that this was one of them. I had been unconscious for several hours at least. They could have easily brought me in through some hidden entrance to the caves and the roundabout tunnels I had been brought through after waking could easily have been to confuse me, make me think I was in some hidden city outside the gates—when all the time I was still inside the caves.

He watched me while I thought over exactly what to say. . . and what not to say, his expression becoming more strained by the minute. Only when I was certain his patience was stretched as far as it would go—did I answer, very careful to keep my answer vague.

“I did not miss them on purpose. . . not entirely anyway. I was delayed. It was only when I saw there was no way I could reach them in time that I decided it would be better to run away and try to find shelter.” I stopped myself a moment, trying to decide if I should let him know I had already been aware of the city's existence or not.

“And the reason you came so close to our hidden city. . . in the dark?" Something in his expression told me he knew it was not by chance—so I told the truth. Most certainly the Chancellor already knew we had seen the city on an earlier outing. If this man was working for the chancellor, he would know it too.

"We had seen it from a distance on a hunting trip. I figured it was my best shot at survival." I shrugged as I spoke, working to make my answer sound as nonchalant as possible.

He nodded and there was something in his eyes that told me that was the answer he had been hoping for. "That's what I thought." He stood then, walking over to an imposing desk that stood just behind the arrangement of chairs and couches and pressed a button before walking back to where I sat. A moment later the door behind me opened and someone walked into the room with quiet footsteps.

"Maggie will see to you, take you down to get a bite to eat, and then show you to where you'll be staying until we find you a more permanent situation. I would suggest eating lightly for now. The blow you took was enough to leave behind a mild concussion. Food may not sit well on your stomach. The med tech suggested light meals for at least eighteen hours. Shouldn't be too hard since you'll sleep at least half of it."

He looked over my shoulder to the person standing behind me then. "I'll send word for the kitchen to fix up a few snacks for her to take with her."

I stood slowly, well aware of how precarious my balance was at the moment and determined not to show him how wobbly I felt. Cautiously, I turned to look at the person behind us as he spoke. She was a tall, slender young woman with drawn features and ramrod straight posture. She stood silently, only nodding her head sharply in response to his instructions.

"We'll talk again soon." The muscles in my back and neck tensed when his hand unexpectedly came around my shoulders. He must have attributed it to my injuries because he lightened his touch as we moved away from the seating area and toward the door, but he did not move his arm. "When you're feeling more up to an in-depth interview."

Something about the way he said "in-depth" worried me. *According to him, they already know a lot about me. . . and they've been watching me. How much more in-depth does he need to be?*

When we reached the door, Maggie nodded to me, then turned and walked out into the hall without a word. I followed, noticing right away that the hall we were in was different. *She must have turned the other way.*

I looked around as we walked. These corridors were enough the same as what I'd been brought through earlier to resemble a maze. I knew there was little chance I would be able to find my way back here without help. . . much less back to where I had started—and since I had no idea where I had been before regaining consciousness, there was little to no chance of finding my way out without help.

"Where is it we're we going exactly?" There was no answer to my question, no gesture or sign that she had even heard me. She just kept walking and I followed—until we reached the end of the hallway, which opened up into an enormous room.

It took several seconds for my eyes to adjust to the change in lighting. The lighting in the hallway we had just come through had seemed a bit dim, but there were lights absolutely everywhere in front of me. Having seen the crazy amount of stars that lit up the sky at night, I thought for a moment that we must be outside, but the warmth of the air around us would surely make that impossible.

I looked around, marveling at the amount of light and heat that existed in such a cavernous room. As my eyes adjusted, I could see that the room around me was indeed cavernous; however, that comparison ended with the size. The far edges were made up of row upon row of open hallways with doors every few feet. Each door had a light in front of it, hanging from the ceiling overhead. And there were more lights hanging from the metal railings that ran the length of each level.

The floor beneath us resembled rock, but everything else I could see was either metal or wood, with each balcony-like hallway appearing to be a type of catwalk, the metal crisscrossed instead of solid. The ceiling was so high, I could only make out a pattern of lights that was far too uniform to be stars—telling me that we must either be underground or in a very tall building.

There were very few people in sight—and when I looked in the direction they were all moving, I spotted Maggie standing a few feet away, looking slightly bored. . . or possibly annoyed. I took a last, quick look around and then walked toward her. She waited until I was within a few feet and then started walking.

We followed the line of people who were entering another hallway—which more closely resembled a tunnel from this side of it. The sounds of talking and laughing floated back to me from the group in front of Maggie, but she still said nothing. I was reminded of the mysterious master-at-arms from the caves, which brought Jude. . . and Adam and Sophia and Sierra and the rest of the class to mind.

Thinking of Jude. . . and my mother and grandparents, was by far the most painful experience so far. They would assume I was dead. It was what we were all taught so why would they think any differently—especially if the class went out to hunt and found no sign of me anywhere.

If they're even allowed back out. I felt certain that the class would look for me if they were allowed back out to hunt. . . especially Jude. *He will not give up on me so easily.* There was a sharp pain in my chest at the thought of never being able to see him again—and I felt tears welling up unexpectedly, heavy in my eyes, but I blinked them away.

I will not show weakness here. Especially if this turns out to be some sort of trap, I cannot afford to put anyone else in danger. Ruthlessly, I shoved all thoughts of Jude to the back corner of my mind.

Fortunately, Maggie didn't stop or turn before I managed to rein in my emotions, though I had only just gotten myself under control when the tunnel opened into another enormous room, albeit not quite as cavernous. I tried to look around as I walked behind her, determined not to lose sight of Maggie or the group of people we had followed here.

The room bore an unsettling resemblance to the dining hall in the caves, tables of all sizes set up in a circular configuration, each one surrounded by chairs; some full, some empty. The walls and ceiling here resembled rock, not metal—telling me we were underground now. . . or at the very least inside a mountain. There was a tightening in my stomach as I thought about what that might mean. Was it possible this really was a part of the caves I had never seen? And if it was. . . why? Why hide living quarters and a dining area? What reason could there be for such a thing?

The only other explanation was too ridiculous to even consider; that this was another network of caves, camouflaged by the crumbling ruins of a city; hidden away in plain sight. . . *or at least plain sight of anyone unlucky enough to find that blasted city.* None of it made any sense to my befuddled brain and I decided it would be best left alone for now since thinking about it was making the ache in my head worse.

A few people looked at me with odd expressions as we passed their tables, but no one spoke—at least to me. I could hear people whispering behind me as I continued to follow Maggie toward the far end of the room—which again had a significant resemblance to the lines where we had picked up our food for communal meals. Though the area was behind a door, the inside looked just the same; long rows of metal tables protected by glass in front and a metal shelf above, lines of people carrying trays moving along in front of them in a stop and start procession.

Maggie walked away from the lines of people, over to another area off to the side where a woman waited just inside a doorway with two trays of food and a small bag. She handed Maggie the first tray without a word, but with a tired smile. Then she turned to me as Maggie stepped to the side.

“Alexander called down. The med techs said you need small meals and food that's going to be easy on your stomach. You won't find anything like that in the food we're serving tonight so I made you up a special tray.” She handed the tray to me before adding, “We'll be celebrating for three days so you have plenty of time to enjoy the feast foods.”

I looked behind me to the lines of people. Though I didn't get a good look at any of the food specifically, the smells that hung in the air were heavenly. My stomach grumbled in reaction.

“Plenty of time. Really. You don't want to spend your night bent over a bucket.” With that, she motioned for me to lift my arm. When I did, she slipped the bag up over my arm, settling it on my shoulder. “There are five small packets in there. Don't eat more than what's in each one at a time and wait at least ninety minutes between them.”

“I will. Thank you.”

She waved a hand at me. “No need. It's my pleasure. Feeding folks is what I do best. Now, you go find a quiet table, maybe off to the edge." She turned toward Maggie when she spoke of finding a table—before turning back to me. "Go. Eat. Rest. It won't be long you'll get to take it easy. Everyone around here pulls their weight." And with that, she waved us away.

I turned as she stepped back through the doorway, the door slowly swinging shut behind her, and followed Maggie out into the large dining area again. She headed for the tables closer to the far end of the room. Past the area where we had come in, there was a group of tables in another section separated from the rest of the room by a wide walkway. Maggie made her way to these, choosing a table with only four seats right at the edge of the section. She set her tray down, then settled herself and started eating.

I watched her for a second before sitting down across from her. Looking at my own tray, I could see that I had been given small portions of foods that would be easy to digest. Thankful for this consideration, I took a bite, hoping the food wouldn't upset my already-nauseous stomach.

SIX

Hope City

Year 45 A.E.

Day I73

I had taken perhaps two bites of food when someone plopped down into the seat next to me, sliding their tray onto the table in front of them as they did. I looked up to see a young woman with bright, curly red hair that was pulled into a messy ponytail—though there were strands escaping all over.

"Hey, you're new, right?"

I nodded in response, since I had a mouth full of food.

She stuck out a hand and then she went on, talking so fast I could barely keep up. "I'm Sandy. When did you get here?

Have you had a tour yet? Where are you staying? Are you in the stacks or the bunks or do you know yet? Hey, why do you have different food? What's that about? Dry toast, mashed potatoes, chicken. . . that's boring stuff. You really don't want to miss out on the feast foods. They don't come around that often. Want some of mine?"

She slid her tray toward me, but before I could say a word, she pulled it back quickly. "Are you allergic or something?" I couldn't help myself. I laughed.

She leaned back in her seat, an odd expression on her face, so I waved a hand and swallowed so I could explain myself. "I'm sorry. I'm not laughing at you. The question was just so unexpected and it's been a very odd day."

"Oh. Okay." was all she said—as I rushed to explain more.

"I would love to try some of the feast foods. Honestly, it looks better than anything I've ever had." She started to push her tray towards me again, a hesitant smile on her face, so I went on quickly. "I can't. The med techs said I have to eat this kind of food for at least eighteen hours and in really small portions."

"Wh. . ." She started to ask and I broke in. "I have a concussion." I winced at the word, memories of my last concussion still so very fresh. "Evidently I was too close to the city and someone felt it best to knock me out so they could get me here safely."

With that, she leaned back again, her mouth a wide "O" of surprise. "You're. . . You. . . Oh wow! I can't. . . I'll be back!" And with that, she bounced off the seat and rushed away. I looked over at Maggie, expecting her to look as confused as I was, but the expression on her face was certainly not one of surprise or shock. It was closer to anger. . . or at the very least, strong annoyance.

"What was all that about?" But she said nothing to answer, directing her attention to her food.

I looked up and tried to figure out where the very talkative Sandy had disappeared to, but could not see her anywhere among the crowd. With another look over at Maggie, I decided I had better take advantage of the momentary quiet to eat what I could of my food before Sandy reappeared—possibly with other talkative people in tow. I tried to eat slowly—even though I knew Sandy would return at some point—because though I had not heard the Med Techs' advice personally, I remembered how food had affected me after my last concussion. It had been days before I'd been able to stomach my normal meals.

Of course, no one had worried quite this much over my

*condition then.*I had been given regular portions and the same food as everyone else each day. Looking back, I was glad Adam had sat with us every day. He had happily taken my extra food and some of Jude's too. Even squirreling some away for later each meal, I'd had leftovers on my tray every meal for days.

I had just taken the last bite of my food when Sandy skidded to a halt beside me, a crowd of at least ten people behind and beside her. "See. Told you!" She was saying.

"That's not her. You're cracked, Sandy." A tall, blond boy beside her spoke, his voice full of disbelief.

"Yeah, she doesn't look a thing like her." This came from a short girl with brown braids hanging over each shoulder.

"But you guys are forgetting, we usually see her all bundled up in arctic gear, with weapons and an enormous pack slung over her back." Another redhead spoke up—and I wondered if she might be related to Sandy. There might have been a slight resemblance, but examining her features closely was giving me a headache so I stopped.

I wanted to ask what they were talking about, who they thought I was, especially when something the man in the office had said to me came to mind; that they watched everything that happened near the caves. Had these people been watching me? Was I the one they thought I was? What was so impressive about me?

I told myself it couldn't be. *They must be thinking of Sierra or Sophia. They're both more impressive than me.*

"Did you really take down that tiger or was it some sort of trick?" The question was very quiet and I didn't immediately know who asked, but the others in the group all turned to look at the smallest person in the crowd, a waifish girl with brown hair. . . that she was wearing in exactly the same style I usually had mine. *Except for now of course.*

I took a second to look around and realized that several of the girls in the group and at least one of the boys were wearing messy ponytails, braided at the end—and realized that they must mean me—and they had to have been watching more than just my activities in the woods by the caves. If they were imitating my hair, they had to have seen me some time without my winter gear.

What is going on around here?

I opened my mouth to ask, but the young girl's question still hung heavily in the air so I answered her first. "I made the shot, but it was really a group effort." The entire group let out a mass gasp, and then they were immediately peppering me with questions, all talking so fast I couldn't have hoped to hear them all. Snippets caught my attention, but that was all—until there was a loud banging sound on the table behind us.

I cringed, surprised that the sudden, ringing noise caused more discomfort to my aching head than the jumble of questions a moment before. The group in front of me fell completely silent and I turned to glare at Maggie. I had heard the man tell her I had a concussion. She had made a point to find a seat away from the main group, in a much quieter area, so why would she make such a racket now?

But the glare had no chance to form. When I turned, there was an older woman standing beside Maggie, someone with an air of authority. This was not a woman you argued with. A shiver went through me at her resemblance to the Chancellor, not just in presence but in features as well. It was almost like looking at a female version of the man himself.

"That's enough. Back to your dinners now." was all she said—and her voice astounded me. Her words held the unmistakeable ring of command, but her tone was surprisingly gentle, motherly, even affectionate.

There was a light scrape from beside me and the sounds of shuffling feet from behind, but I kept my eyes trained on her face, looking for any sign that this was some sort of trick to lull me into a false complacency.

"How about I take it from here, Maggie." Her voice was still kind, almost motherly, but that underlying authority was still very present. I turned to Maggie, almost hoping she would protest. For some undefinable reason, I found that I did not want to be alone with this woman, but Maggie said nothing. She nodded and turned to leave, taking her empty tray with her.

Once she had gone, I turned back to face the woman, half expecting her demeanor to change completely, but she gave no indication of change, sitting gracefully in front of the tray I'd not noticed before.

“Do you mind waiting? I haven't had a bite all afternoon.” Her voice still held a note of authority, but there was something else threaded through her words now as well, something that sounded suspiciously like the exhaustion I had heard in my mother's voice all too often. Without thinking, I muttered my assent and collapsed back into my own chair, feeling the fatigue in myself now that the excitement earlier had somehow masked.

Several minutes passed in silence as she ate. I took the opportunity to study her. The more I looked, the more obvious her resemblance to the Chancellor became, but there was no sensible explanation for it that I could think of. I had almost convinced myself I was imagining it, or that my concussed mind was somehow making me imagine the resemblance because of my own fears, or perhaps even that I had just died and this was a very strange sort of afterlife, when she stopped eating and looked up at me.

"Do we need to get you more pain medication?" Her question took me so completely by surprise, that I stumbled over my words for a few seconds before answering simply. "No, why?"

"You look as if you're in pain."

"Oh! No, that's not it at all." I was so relieved that she had not somehow figured out what I had been doing at the time, that I blurted out more than I meant to. "I was just trying to make sense of all this."

She nodded. "Yes, it is a lot to take in. And with a concussion, things must feel a bit surreal to you as well."

I could think of no safe answer so I just nodded in response, and after a moment she went on. "No doubt Alexander felt it would be better to explain things to you later, after you are feeling better, but I am willing to wager that you have a million questions." She spoke with a certainty, as if from experience. I found myself wondering if she had once lived in the caves herself and perhaps had somehow landed here somewhat by surprise as well.

She finished chewing before continuing. "I can practically see the gears turning in that head of yours. To answer the obvious question, yes, I was born in the caves. I won't bore you with all of the details, but suffice it to say that I ended up here as a young woman and I have never for one moment regretted it. Now," She pushed her empty tray aside and went on. "Are there any questions I can answer for you."

I couldn't help it. It might have been the concussion, or it might have been my own curiosity just getting the better of me, but I launched into several questions that had been bothering me since I woke up on a hard, cold table in a brightly-lit room. "Why do all of those kids seem to know exactly who I am and how I ended up here? Who is this Alexander everyone keeps talking about? For that matter, who are you and why did everyone scatter just because you told them to? What is the feast everyone keeps talking about? And why doesn't Maggie talk. . . ever?" I finished in a huff of breath and took several deep breaths, the sudden throbbing in my head almost too much for me to handle at the moment.

"I'll just start at the beginning, shall I?" She spoke quietly, for which I was grateful since in my rush to ask all of my questions at once, I had inadvertently made the pain in my head tremendously worse.

"Those kids know who you are because several of them are part of the surveillance team who are responsible for watching the monitors and reporting about what goes on near the caves. They've seen you in action quite a lot lately and I am afraid that once word of you taking down the great snowy tiger got around, well, let us say that they are no longer the only fans you have here."

"Great snowy tiger? That's what you call it? I don't understand why that is so impressive. I was just doing my job —and it was a lucky shot."

"Lucky?" There was disbelief in her expression and her tone.

"Yes, lucky. Of course, since I've never run across another one, I couldn't prove that if I wanted to. And none of that explains why they knew how I got here."

"I believe Sandy was on duty when it went down. If it makes you feel any better, she isn't speaking to Matteo because he hit you—and since they've been attached at the hip since I've known them, that is saying something." Knowing someone held this Matteo responsible for his behavior actually did make me feel a bit better, but she went on before I could say anything.

"Alexander is our leader. He prefers a very informal relationship with everyone, given the terror he endured at the hands of your Chancellor—and his system seems to work quite well. He has a way of making everyone feel like family. My name is Astrid and I assist Alexander in various ways around." Her smile tightened a little, but her tone did not change as she went on. "I presume the kids scattered because they tend to be afraid of me. Most of the adults understand that I am nothing like my brother, but I suppose it's just not something Sandy and her crew can stomach, though I keep trying anyway." She said this last with a slight shrug, her smile turning sad as she finished speaking.

I took the opportunity to break in. "Who is your brother and why would it matter if you're anything like him or not?" Suddenly a theory about her resemblance to the Chancellor was not so crazy. If he was her brother. . . My thoughts were interrupted by her answer. "It's not really important who my brother is. What is important is that I am nothing like him, because he is not a very nice person." And her refusal to name him was nearly all the evidence I needed. I was tempted to voice my suspicions, but she chose that moment to continue with answering my earlier questions.

"The feast is a three day celebration we have every winter at this time. It combines as many of the ancient traditions of Hanukkah, Christmas and several other less well-known holidays that used to take place as we can possibly fit into three days. We have special meals all three days and everyone's work hours are cut significantly so that they all have time to enjoy the special activities that take place in the stacks and the great hall. I don't know how much you will feel up to participating, considering your concussion, but it really is great fun."

"Maggie was supposed to show me where I will be sleeping until a more permanent spot is figured out. Will she still be doing that or. . . will you?" At the mention of Maggie, Astrid's smile disappeared entirely.

"Yes, about Maggie. You asked why she never speaks. She had an accident as a child. I will not go in to the details, but her entire family was involved and it must have been quite traumatic for her because she has not said a word since."

"So, she can speak? She just doesn't?" Her story was reminding me more and more of the mysterious master-at-arms from the caves.

"As far as we know, she can. There is no medical reason the Med Techs can find that explains her lack of speech. We have also never been able to decipher whether or not she is withdrawn because she is sensitive about not speaking or if it is simply leftover trauma from losing her entire family." Something about the way she said it told me this was all the information I was going to get out of her about this subject so I made a mental note to ask Sandy the next time I saw her. She seemed like someone who knew everything about everyone around here.

“As for showing you to your quarters, there has actually been a more permanent situation presented for you. Alexander did not take your fan club into account when he asked Maggie to take you to the bunks.” She hesitated a moment, her lips twitching as she looked at the crowded room behind me.

“When he sent word for a place to be prepared for you there, the messenger—who happens to be a close friend of Sandy's—approached me about the situation. She was certain your presence there would cause quite a commotion, so together we went in search of a roommate for you. As it happens, there is a young lady about your age who just lost hers. We approached her and she is amenable to giving it a try.”

“A try?” I asked, not entirely certain I wanted to know the answer.

“Yes, a try. I am sad to say that she is not the easiest person to get along with. She's had five different roommates in the two years since we moved her out of the bunks. Of course, her latest roommate married so that's hardly her fault.”

Something about the way she said it told me there was more to the story, but I didn't press. Instead, I focused on something else she had said. "Married? What does that mean?" Something about the word was oddly familiar, but I couldn't quite place why. . . or what it meant.

Astrid shook her head a little. "Sorry. I forgot. It's very similar to what you know as binding. Here in Hope City, the traditional phrase never went out of fashion."

I was nodding my head before she finished answering. Her connecting the two words had brought to mind why the phrase was so familiar to me. It was one of the things my grandparents had taught me as a younger child. It was also one of the things they had not shared with every other child in the groups they taught.

"If you're finished. . ." As she stood and picked up her own, she motioned to my empty tray. "We'll go and get you settled."

"Sure." I lifted my tray, slung the bag with food for later over my shoulder, and followed her.

SEVEN

Hope City

Year 45 A.E.

Day I74

The combination of surprise and nausea woke me—as I struggled to move away from the person who was shaking me. . . hard.

"Hey, are. . ." She stopped when I pushed my way off the bed and rushed for the bathroom, grateful I had familiarized myself with the small compartment earlier when Astrid had left me here, saying something about finding my new roommate.

I had slowly explored the small space, annoyed at just how

many times I'd had to stop and balance myself against walls and counters. The space was much larger than I had expected, larger in a lot of ways than the tiny compartment our family had shared in the caves, though in some ways it might also have been considered more cramped.

There were two bedrooms of similar size, long and thin, with a wide, shallow closet that ran the length of the inner wall and was sectioned carefully into areas to hang clothing, plus drawers and shelves to stack shoes and the like. It was obvious that whoever had put the rooms together had taken the lack of space into consideration, from the closet that was designed with everything one might need to store clothes and personal items, to the rooms themselves. Every piece of furniture was attached in some way to a wall, those connections serving as legs and hinges at the same time. The bed had actually been folded up against the wall—and it had taken several false starts before I managed to figure out how to fold it down.

There was one bathroom, attached to both bedrooms, but also to the hallway that ran the width of the square kitchen. The main room was—like the bedrooms—narrow and long. However, the furniture in the main room was freestanding and grouped loosely in a conversation area, with two overstuffed chairs next to one wall that contained floor to ceiling shelves that were filled with books. . . more books than I had ever seen in one place.

I had a moment to be grateful there was no need to wait for the bathroom fixtures to appear. If that had been the case, I was certain I would have made a mess everywhere. Fortunately, it was not the case and I merely dropped to my knees as the violent retching took over, each wave causing another until I was certain I had emptied the contents of my stomach at least a dozen times.

When the sickness finally passed, I leaned back against the cool metal of the wall, desperate for the turbulence in my head to settle before my stomach reacted violently again.

"Are you all right?" The voice surprised me, obviously not Astrid. . . or anyone else I had spoken to so far. I started to move my head to look up at the person who must be my new roommate, but the slightest movement sent a nearly unbearable shaft of pain through my head and had my stomach muscles clenching in anticipation of the sickness that was trying to overwhelm me again.

"Is there anything I can do—anything I can get you?" The question was another surprise. Was this truly the young woman whom Astrid had said had difficulty with her roommates in the past? I wanted to ask, but was afraid to open my mouth—and I knew moving my head would be the wrong choice. The only option I could think of was a wave.

It took all the energy I could muster, just to flutter my fingers a little. The weakness made me want to scream, and the threat of more sickness made me want to cry.

Jude, where are you when I really need you? Dozens of thoughts and memories rushed through my mind, more than dizzying as they swirled and jumbled around in my already unsteady head. It was nearly painful to remember how careful he had been with me the last time I had experienced a concussion—even while being severely injured himself. It was more than I could take in the moment and I did not have the strength to fight the hot tears that were suddenly coursing down my cheeks.

I barely registered the movement as someone stepped over me, too weak to care anymore if someone witnessed the vulnerability I had barely even allowed myself to acknowledge. A moment later, the sound of water running in the metal sink reached my ears and I found—after a moment—that if I concentrated on the soothing flow, the chaotic sickness in my head calmed a little.

Testing myself, I took several deep breaths—just as someone placed a cool, damp cloth gently against my forehead. Something about the movement unleashed a fresh torrent of tears and my breath broke on a harsh sob.

“You must have loved him very much.”

I didn't even try to argue, knowing it would be ridiculous to try. The misery in her voice told me she knew exactly how I felt. There was no judgement in her voice or her words, just the shared agony of losing the one person who had taken hold in your heart.

The air shifted as she slid to the floor beside me and gently placed an arm around my shoulders. For the first time since I had awoken in this place, I allowed the misery and anguish to pour out—and when the wracking sobs did not churn up a new bout of nausea in my stomach, I could not help but wonder how much of the queasiness had actually been due to holding in all of this pain.

There was no way to determine just how long I sat there on the cold, hard floor, leaning against this woman who I couldn't even be certain was my new roommate. But when the sobs finally began to slow and the tears dried on my cheeks, she spoke softly—and I was shocked to hear a break in her voice.

“I won't lie to you and tell you it gets easier because the truth is it never does.” She was quiet for what felt like several minutes before she went on. “But eventually you will be able to handle it better.” Her voice was very quiet, her words barely a whisper of sound.

It was more than obvious that she knew precisely how I was feeling, and I felt certain it must be because she had been through the same experience of losing the one she loved. It was an odd feeling, the strength of connection I felt. . . to this person I didn't even know, the camaraderie of shared experience. . . and shared pain.

"How long has it been?" The words startled me. It was not at all what I had meant to ask—and it felt far too intimate.

The silence stretched out and I was ready to retract the words and beg forgiveness—when she answered, her voice still hardly more than a whisper. "Too long. . . far too long. Ninety-five days." A small light came from somewhere and her next words told me she she must have been checking the time on her digital. "and eight hours." Her voice broke again on the last word and I shifted so I could wrap my arm around her.

It was surprising that the movement sent no nausea through me, but it was also a relief and it gave me the courage to pull myself into a sitting position so that I could wind my other arm around her thin shoulders. She made no sounds, but I could feel the sobs shaking her slightly and a tear landed on my arm, giving her away.

I said nothing, only trying to share the comfort she had given to me only moments before.

Several minutes passed before she spoke again. "Who would've thought that we would bond over such a thing?" Her words were half question, half statement and I felt myself nodding as unexpected laughter bubbled up in my throat. I thought about what Astrid had said earlier about my new roommate being difficult to get along with. *She could not have been further from the truth. . . only she may never know.* Instinctively I knew I should never let on about our shared pain outside of the walls of these rooms—and I was certain she would extend the same courtesy.

I found myself wondering if that might have been one of the issues she'd had with roommates in the past. Either they had spoken of her pain where they should not have. *Or else they were involved with someone and she couldn't bear to watch them together.* Given what Astrid had said about her most recent roommate, that felt like the more accurate assumption.

Or perhaps her last roommate was not not the only one to pair up.

"We should try to get some sleep." She cleared her throat when her voice broke again—and then went on. "It's late." The lightning quick change in mood. . . and tone might have surprised anyone else, but I understood perfectly.

She stood and started to move away before turning back to offer me a hand—which I gratefully took since I was still feeling more weak than I cared to admit. I had no more than gained my footing when she did turn and walk out, leaving me alone. . . for which I was also grateful. I took care of the remains of my one and only meal, having fallen asleep before I could break into one of the meal packets. I carefully wiped down the sink and toilet before washing my hands and face, and strangely, a soothing calm settling over me as I performed the familiar tasks.

When at last I did emerge and went in search of something cool to drink, I was stunned to see that she had waited up. She was sitting at the tiny table attached to the half wall that separated the kitchen area from the main room, her hand wrapped around a small cup. "Feeling better?"

"Yes, thank you." I dropped into the chair across the table from her, thankful for the opportunity to rest before making my way back to the bedroom.

"So, was that the concussion or something else?" Her voice held a note of curiosity, but there was something else underlying in the tone, something that made me wonder just how difficult it would be to get to know this person. . . really get to know her.

"I can't be sure, but I'm going to guess that it was the concussion mostly. Why were you shaking me so hard anyway?"

"You were screaming. At first I thought something else must be wrong, but it didn't take too long to figure out that you were sleeping, dreaming. . . having a nightmare. Waking you up seemed like the best idea at the time. Trust me when I say that you really don't want a lot of attention over something like a dream. People talk." She waved a hand in dismissal, but I was sure I could see a glint of tears in her eyes again. "There isn't a lot of other entertainment, you know."

There was something in her tone that told me Astrid had filled her in on more than just the concussion so I quickly decided that the best option was to go with nonchalance. "Thanks. Yeah, I don't really want a lot of attention. . . or any more at least."

She laughed then for the first time. "Yeah. Good luck with that. Astrid filled me in. You're going to have your hands full with that crowd. They look at you like some sort of hero." She shook her head a little, a half-smile on her face, before going on. "They're going to be following you around like a pack of puppies, all the while hoping some of it will rub off on them."

"Why though? What's special about me? I'm nobody. . .

seriously. . . nobody."

There was a look of respect in her eyes that confused me. Why should she respect me. Hadn't I just said I wasn't a hero? I hadn't really done anything. Not only that, I'd failed to save so many people. And I had left behind the rest of our class, which was probably tantamount to sending them off to their deaths.

Thinking about Anna and Malcolm and Jordan brought tears to my eyes. I tried to be nonchalant as I swiped angrily at them. Fortunately, she either didn't notice or she decided not to comment on it.

"First, you're a hero to them because you've survived not only the caves, but the hunting parties, too."

"Yeah, but that's not really. . ."

But she cut me off. "It is something. You've seen what goes on in those caves. Any hint of rebellion is dealt with swiftly and harshly." There was a shadow in her eyes as she spoke. I almost broke in, but she quickly went on. "And I know you've seen—in the nearly three months you were involved in the hunting parties—how many hunters never come back."

I nodded my head, slowly, solemnly. I had seen, but I certainly didn't think that made me a hero.

"They see something in you that they want from themselves,

in themselves. You've shown them a strength that comes from standing against impossible odds and never backing down. It also doesn't hurt that you're so modest about it all." She said the last with a laugh and I wanted to argue, but she was waving a hand to get my attention. "I'm not laughing at you. I'm laughing at the irony. Caves full of people who think they're the toughest, the strongest, the most amazing—and you're the one who captures the attention."

"Attention I really don't want. . . or need."

"Go figure." She laughed quietly again. There was still a shadow in her eyes, but she didn't look quite so intense now. I started to say something, but she beat me to it. "Coffee?" She motioned to an odd looking contraption on the counter behind her, and instead of answering, I found myself staring at the small machine. It seemed impossible that such a small object could brew coffee.

"Do you drink coffee?" Her question caught me off guard and I blurted out the question in my head instead of an answer. "Are you telling me that thing makes coffee. . . seriously? How does it work?"

She only laughed again. "Right. I forgot. Caves." She said it like that somehow explained everything, but while I sat there, staring, waiting, unsure what to say next, she answered.

"There are so many things here that are nothing like they are there. You'll see. One of them is the coffee."

Looking towards the main room, I added, "and the books."

She smiled then. "Yeah. Isn't it great? Not everyone appreciates reading quite like I do, but at least no one here has a problem with it." When she said nothing else, I asked the other question that had been on my mind since I had seen the shelves.

"Have you read them all?"

"Not yet. I'm working on it though. Maybe about half." She shrugged a little before going on. "But then, I've only been here about three. . ." She trailed off and, after a second, looked down into her half-empty cup.

At a loss, too exhausted to think of something suitable to say, I sat silently. . . until it occurred to me that I still did not even know her name.

"You know. . . it just occurred to me that we haven't been properly introduced."

She laughed and the shadows receded a little from her eyes. "True. But then, you were asleep when I came in and it didn't seem right to wake you." She laughed again before going on. "Until you started screaming, that is." We both laughed.

"Actually, I already know your name, Eve, and I can only hope you find this as humorous as I do." She paused for a moment, but went on before I could say anything. "Oh man, this could get confusing." Curious and a little concerned, I waited—and finally she went on. "My name. . . is Eva."

I couldn't be sure if it was the concussion or the late hour, but I was sure I'd heard her wrong so I asked. "Eva? Really?" She nodded—and when she did. . . when I realized I had heard her right, my only reaction was laughter. . . "You are exactly right. It could get very confusing." And I kept laughing. I just couldn't seem to stop.

After only a second or two, she joined in and we laughed together for several minutes before fatigue started dragging at me. "Okay, yeah... if we're going to be up awhile more, I will definitely need some coffee."

Eva laughed again before adding her own comment. "Yeah, I'm surprised Astrid didn't warn you. You'll have to drink a lot of coffee if you want to keep up with me."

"Oh, so that's why you have your own machine then?" My laughter now was starting to sound odd. . . even to me. The events of the day and the wretched sickness and my over-extended emotions were all churning together to drain me of every last ounce of energy.

"I'm not so sure coffee is what you need now. I think bed is a better answer." She stood—and I pushed myself out of the chair, too tired to be annoyed when I had to lean heavily on the table. A moment later, Eva's arm wrapped around me and then we were moving slowly toward the hallway.

EIGHT

Hope City

Year 45 A.E.

Day I74

The sound of someone whistling was the first thing that registered in my sleep-fogged mind. Though, when I moved, I was thrilled to discover that there was no nausea to fight against. And the pain in my head was even less pronounced.

The next thing that registered was the wonderful smell that must have been a combination of breakfast. . . and coffee. The tantalizing scents were enough to entice me from the comfort and warmth of the thick covers and soft bed.

I swung my legs over the edge of the bed just as Eva appeared in my doorway. "Hey, sleepyhead. How are you feeling this morning?"

"Better, I think." I eased myself up, expecting the world to tilt in strange ways, but everything stayed just as it should so I sat up with a smile. "Definitely better."

"Feeling up to some breakfast? I'm not sure if everything is on the approved list, but you can eat what you think you can handle and leave the rest for later." I nodded absently as I stood and looked to where I had left the outer clothes I'd removed the night before, grateful to find sleepwear folded up on the bed, waiting for me.

I looked down at the pajamas I had pulled on the night before —and then over to where I had left the clothes I'd worn throughout the day. . . folded up neatly in a little pile. . . and the smell of coffee called to me so I followed Eva without changing. "Great. Let's eat."

I walked all the way into the kitchen before I noticed what time it was. It was already after eleven. The morning was almost over. "My goodness. It's late. I never sleep this late."

"Well. . . we were up pretty late, too." Eva answered as she moved around the kitchen, walking to the long counter that held the coffee machine, a cooktop, a wide sink and several machines I didn't recognize. She handed me a plate as she moved along, filling her own plate with delectable looking foods; scrambled eggs, crisp bacon, juicy sausage, fluffy pancakes, and fat muffins. She filled a tall mug with coffee and gestured for me to fill my own plate.

As delicious as everything looked, I wanted to pile my plate high, but knew it would be a mistake, between my stomach being so abused early this morning and the concussion, so I took small portions of each and filled my own mug only half full. Then I moved over to the table and took the seat opposite her, taking a moment to enjoy the delightful smells wafting up from my plate. “How long have you been up?”

She looked up at me, a smile playing at the corner of her lips. “Awhile. Why?”

“Well, you had time to do all of this. Thank you, by the way. I'm not sure I could have found that dining area again this morning.”

She broke in there before I could go on. “They stop serving breakfast at nine so. . .” She shrugged and then added, “Plus, they would have been serving a much more basic breakfast. It's standard during the Winter Feast. They have a fabulous buffet at lunch and go all out for dinner each day so breakfast is only fancy on the first day.” A second later she added, “Sorry.”

I waved a hand in dismissal as I dug into the eggs. “No, it's fine. I wouldn't have been able to enjoy it anyway. . . being unconscious." She looked at me for a full ten seconds before I smiled—and then she laughed. "Good point."

"Mmm. I can't imagine anything better than this, anyway." I hadn't even swallowed completely before I spoke—and she smiled widely in return before applying herself to her own plate.

We ate in companionable silence for a long time, the only sounds in the room an occasional clink of fork against plate. Even though I had started with much less food on my plate than Eva, I had made myself eat slowly so we finished at the same time, both rising at the same time, each clearing our own half of the table. Unsure of how things worked here, I followed her lead; rinsing my plate and mug quickly and turning off the tap before placing both in the cleansing unit below the sink. . . which was smaller than the one in our compartment in the caves, though it looked newer and more advanced.

"Now, we need to get going. There are lots of things going on today and you won't want to miss any of them." She moved out of the kitchen and started toward my room so I followed. *Perhaps one of the things we can do today is find me some more clothes.* I tried to decide how to broach the subject as I moved to where I had laid my clothes the night before.

She spoke before I could make my way over to the neat pile. "You know, you don't have to wear those again." She moved to the closet and opened it to reveal a large box resting on the floor. "I put the box in here last night, but I didn't want to wake you so I just left it there." She carried it over to the bed before I could move forward to help. Then she opened it and started pulling out an array of items, laying them on the bed in piles; shirts and pants, socks and underwear.

I walked over to the bed and ran a finger along the top of one of the piles. Not one item she had pulled out so far was plain or shapeless, like our clothing in the caves. There was a rainbow of colors, mostly earthy tones, but all unexpectedly rich and vibrant—and each item she pulled out was more stylish than anything I had ever owned. Then I looked over at what Eva was wearing. The cut, design and fabrics were very similar to what she was pulling out of the box that was supposedly for me. The colors were softer, more muted, but no less vibrant and obviously stylish.

"Are you sure these are supposed to be for me?" There were several shirts and thin jackets that reminded me more of what the Chancellor's aides had been wearing when they had escorted us to a very fancy part of the caves to inform us of Anna's death. Everyone there had been dressed nicer than any of us in the main sections of the caves. And Eva just kept pulling things out.

“Yes, I'm sure. Everyone who comes here from the caves shows up with pretty much nothing, and they issue these starter boxes. Why?” She looked up at me as she answered and something in my expression must have answered her question because she went on without my saying anything. “Right. . . Yeah. They're nothing like what you wear in the caves.” And she went back to pulling items out.

“And don't worry. . . If any of these are not your taste, just put them in one pile and leave it out. Later I'll show you where we trade. You'll have starter credits, but trading out clothes is usually an even swap.” She shrugged and added. “Unless you need something special, anyway.” She looked over at the clothes I had laid over the small stool I'd pulled out from under the desk. “They must have given you those when you woke up because they're definitely not outdoor wear.”

I nodded, answering absently. “Yeah. I'm not sure what they did with the clothes I was wearing. They gave me these to put on when I woke up.” A moment later, she pulled my coat out of the box and then several other items that I had been wearing, obviously clean, but well-worn—and something about the sight of them had my chest tightening with emotion. “Well, these aren't new. They must be. . .” She stopped when she turned and looked at me. A moment later she had abandoned the box and wrapped her arms around me. "It's okay. Really. Let it out or you'll end up giving yourself a headache again." Shame stopped the tears for several very long seconds before they broke free, rushing down my cheeks in a hot torrent of harsh release. "I. . ." my voice broke on a sob and I stopped fighting the emotion that was battering me when pain shot through my head. . . just as Eva had predicted.

"I know it doesn't help—and it probably sounds trite, but I went through this exact same thing when I came here." Her confession distracted me just enough that I was able to get my crazed emotions back under control a little.

"When you came here?" I asked, stepping back and thinking over her words from earlier about others coming here from the caves. Did this happen a lot then? "You came here from the caves? How? Why? When?"

She let out a short laugh before answering. "Ninety-five days. . . remember?" And in my mind I was doing the math, counting back to try and think of when a young woman had gone missing. I didn't recognize her so it must have been before I had signed up to train as a hunter. I raised a hand to cover the gasp that escaped when the timing clicked into place in my head.

"You were. . . Then they all. . . Are they. . ."

She was already nodding. "Yes, they rescued us. Though there were a few who didn't make it. Their injuries. . ." She trailed off there, but shook herself a second later. "Some of the kids had it much worse than others—and it's not like anyone in there is in excellent health, anyway." She shrugged again, but there was something in her voice, something cold, hard, frightening, a moment later when she added, "except the Chancellor's people, that is."

I wanted to ask who had been in such bad shape, but it was still so new to her—and it felt like maybe someone who didn't make it had meant a lot to her.

She turned back to the box and went back to pulling things out, her movements jerky and stiff. I took the opportunity to pick up several things and examine them more closely. The things she had pulled out didn't look suitable for the hard work several people had inferred we would be doing to pull our weight in the caves—and I found myself wondering just what they had in mind for me.

Of course, I've always got the clothes they gave me yesterday. There was nothing fancy about the plain pants, shirt and serviceable jacket I had removed last night. Perhaps those were meant to be work clothes and the others were for another purpose that would be revealed at a later time.

"Oh good. They did think of it." Just then, Eva pulled two long white boxes out of the larger box. "Now where. . . Oh! Good." She pulled out another long, thin box and set it beside the others, turning to me a moment later with only a slightly stiff smile on her delicate features. "I was worried we would have to rush off right now and take care of this." She turned back then and opened one of the boxes, shaking the folds out of a long, thin shimmery sheath of material. Only when she turned to me and held it up between us, did I realize it was a dress. . . and a fancy one at that; with a neckline that sent butterflies dancing in my stomach and a design that looked like it would drape and cling to every curve.

"Yes, this will do nicely." She walked toward me, holding the dress up to my shoulders, as if she were imagining just how I would look wearing it. After a minute she nodded and stepped back, but said nothing. I wanted to object, but no words came to me as I continued to study the piece of clothing she obviously expected me to wear at some point. What reason could there possibly be for me to wear such a thing?

"I'm guessing you've never worn heels." I could only shake my head in answer. Something told me she meant heels like the Chancellor's assistant had been wearing. . . not the slightly elevated heels like those on my hunting boots—and the butterflies were suddenly dancing crazily, stirring up fresh nausea, and joined by a slight sense of dizziness in my head.

If there were any outward signs of my panic, she paid no attention to them, waving a hand in dismissal before saying. "We have until tomorrow night. That's plenty of time." She walked over to the closet and hung up the dress before returning to the bed and opening the smaller, squarer box, pulling out a pair of shoes with a much more conservative heel than I had been expecting. And I was also relieved to see that they were black, not the same shimmering silver as the dress she had just hung up. She handed them to me.

"Give them a try. See if they fit. Otherwise, we might need to trade them out."

While she walked back to the bed, I set the shoes carefully on the floor in front of me and then put a foot into the first one, torn between relief and disappointment when it fit my foot perfectly. I might tell myself that I could find a way to switch them out for a shoe that had less height, but the sheer possibility of ending up with a pair that sported the ridiculously tall, impossibly thin stick like those on the boots worn by the Chancellor's assistant made me think it might be best to just let it be.

Getting my foot into the other shoe proved most difficult as I had nothing to hold onto and my balance was not accustomed to the shift in weight that occurred with my heels forced two inches off the ground higher than I was used to. In the end, I took the first shoe off and carried both over closer to the desk, using the edge to stabilize myself as I slipped on the first and then the second shoe.

"Those are great." I looked up to see her moving over to the hook by the closet I hadn't noticed before with my heavy coat. She hung it there and moved back to the bed to pick up the clothing that had obviously been cleaned and then put with everything new. "You want these, right?" She waited for my answer, but all I could do was nod.

Eva nodded in return and moved to place them in the closet while I slipped my feet carefully out of the fancy shoes. "Now, you need to look over these other things and tell me if there is anything you're going to want to trade. We can do that easily enough this afternoon. I looked at the piles of fine things covering my bed and didn't see a single thing that didn't frighten me. "I'm guessing everything else I could trade for would be pretty much this fancy though?"

She laughed before answering. "Don't worry. You'll get used to it." She turned to pick up several items she had obviously put together for me to wear. "Here. These are just fancy enough for the day's events—hopefully without being too overwhelming for you." She handed me the clothes and then moved back to the piles on the bed.

With no more arguments, I carried the clothes into the bathroom and changed, marveling at how different they felt against my skin than the scratchy, itchy, rough fabrics I had spent most of my life in. The pants were thick, but soft and they fit comfortably without being too tight or loose. The shirt was thick, warm, and soft as a cloud. Even the socks were more comfortable than any I had ever worn.

When I walked out of the bathroom, she stood there with a pair of brown ankle boots dangling from her hand. I cringed when I saw that they had a heel that looked more fashionable than functional. "You really want me to walk around in those all day? It might not be pretty."

She only laughed and handed the boots to me. "Come on. These are not bad. . . not at all. I know you can handle them."

Thinking of the shoes she expected me to walk in soon, I realized I had better get in some practice. "Fine." I acquiesced and took the shoes, moving over to the bed to put them on.

"Good. Okay. I'll be back." And with that, she was gone. From the sound of her footsteps, she went to her own room, presumably to finish getting herself ready. I sat on the bed to pull the new boots into place and laced them tightly, hesitantly getting to my feet—and pleasantly surprised when they held firm under my weight. I took several small, slow steps to test my balance, arms stretched out on either side and I was delighted to find that I was not in the least wobbly. Walking felt different than I was used to and I could feel a pull in unfamiliar muscles, but the experience was not as unpleasant as I had been anticipating.

"You ready?" Eva appeared in the doorway just then. "Yeah. Those will do nicely. Come on." I turned to follow and noticed that she had changed part of her outfit; switching out her flat shoes for heeled boots that hugged her calves and ended just under her knees. She had also added a short leather jacket with a wide belt that ended in an oversized buckle that hung loose in front. "This is going to be fun."

I started to say something about how she should know, when I realized this would be Eva's first Winter Feast as well. "Hey, you've only been here three months. How do you know so much about how the all this stuff goes?"

"Oh, I've seen footage from previous years. It's easier than asking people about it." Her smile was equal parts pride and mischief when she answered, but it disappeared quickly and she went on, her voice now full of worry. "Oh! Please don't tell anyone about that."

I shook my head. "Of course not." and added a moment later, "You must have a pretty important job."

She shrugged before answering. "Not really. It's mostly sitting at a desk and watching a screen while wearing this huge, unattractive headset and trying to stay awake." And then she was pulling me out the door. "Come on, let's go check this thing out."

Walking from the dining area last evening, I had caught a glimpse of the tables and tents set up in the open area below the stacks; the main living area. . . where our compartment and hundreds of others were, but I had not had the energy or the inclination to stop and explore. Not to mention, I'd had no idea at that point where to go to find our compartment. I had merely followed Astrid, who had escorted me to the door, shown me that my thumbprint was my key, and then said something about finding my roommate and rushed off. If she had returned, I would never have known, having fallen asleep after a quick look through the compar. . . no, apartment—Eva said they were called apartments in the city.

Now I was here among the Winter Celebration setup. As we walked, Eva pointed out things to me; places I could go to get the things I might need. More than a few tables and tents among the open area held clothing, shoes and other personal items. There were also people displaying artwork, books, and all sorts of trinkets. Eva stopped at two different tents with books and I spent a few minutes exploring the selection. I'd not had much time yet to peruse her collection, but I saw several titles that caught my attention and found myself hoping she had them already.

Our next stop was one of the tables displaying treats Eva said you could only find at that one place. "A tip from one of the guys in my work section," she told me quietly while the proprietor was still helping another patron. "He said this woman was the only one who knows how to make these things. Some recipe handed down through her family for hundreds of years."

When it was our turn, Eva made the excuse of demonstrating how the credit system worked by buying treats for both of us. I gave her actions the proper amount of attention, though it was hardly a difficult system—using the same technique as the door to our apartment—and I made no arguments about insisting on using my own credits for my treat since it was obvious she was intent on being generous.

We had barely moved three feet before Eva bit into her pastry.

Watching her enjoyment, I bit into my own, sighing as the exquisite flavors danced on my tongue. The pastry was absolutely perfect in every way; soft and fluffy, covered in what appeared to be a softer form of sugar than I had ever seen.

Licking the cream from our lips and fingers, Eva and I made our way to the next table. . . and then the next, walking slowly and looking over the items displayed at each one.

NINE

Hope City

Year 45 A.E.

Day I74

We had passed several tables and two tents before Eva made another stop. "Do you mind? I've been needing a new belt for some time now."

I nodded and followed as she walked into the large tent beside us. There were all manner of things displayed inside, from shoes to coats to belts and hats. Some items were hung, some laid out neatly on tables, some draped over tables and benches. While Eva went in search of her belt, I made my way to the back of the tent, my attention fixed on the items hung decoratively on the back wall of the tent.

I was still several feet away when the memory of that first time we had used snow shoes came back to me, and the breath caught in my throat as my mind rushed through the images. . . and the feelings; the bite in the air, the snowball fight, the feeling of Jude's body pressed against mine, the way my heart had pounded when I'd thought he was going to kiss me.

That had been the first time I had ever looked at a boy as anything other than a neighbor. . . or a co-worker.

The same confusion and frustration swirled in me now that I had felt then. I missed Jude so much it hurt. It was killing me to be so far apart. I wanted him here. . . with me. I wanted to know he was safe and out of harm's way. I needed—desperately needed—to touch him, feel his arms around me again, feel his lips on mine.

"You like?" The question pulled me from my thoughts and I shook my head a little, trying to shake away the last traces of heat that had taken hold of me at the memory of kissing Jude. I looked up at the snow shoes again and realized I must have been staring at them.

"I do. Yes. They reminded me of something. . . someone. . ." My voice trailed off with the last word because as I got closer to them, I could see there was something about them that was eerily familiar. "You have used them before?" I nodded in answer, trying to figure out why there was something about the man that was familiar. Something about him that made me feel as if I had met him before.

Of course, after what Eva had said earlier about being rescued from the storm on the night so many children had been forced through the gates. . . out into the storm, I was beginning to look around me with new eyes; searching for other people I might know from the caves. *That could be what is going on here. Perhaps I have seen him before—only I don't remember because he was lost outside the gates at some point.*

"You are a hunter, yes?" His question stopped me, made me wonder just what I would be doing here. I had been a hunter in the caves and obviously someone had been watching me, knew I was good at it. Perhaps they would let me go on doing that—though I had no idea what that would mean here.

"Oh, then you do have hunters here?"

"You are a great hunter." There was an unmistakable pride in his voice that told me he was speaking more from knowledge than from the look of me. He must have seen some of the surveillance footage Sandy and her friends were so intrigued by.

“I was, yes.”

“You will be again. You must have patience.” He nodded, and patted my arm; much in the same way my grandfather would have—which brought unexpected tears to me eyes.

I mumbled something about looking around and turned quickly, struggling to keep my emotions in check. It would certainly not do to break down right here in this tent. . . at the Winter Feast, with so many people celebrating around me. I wandered over to a display he had with what looked like weapon sheaths. There were dozens of different sizes, designs and types of them; some for knives, some obviously for swords, and several that looked like the quiver I had kept my arrows in from the caves.

“Is there actually somewhere around here we can buy weapons?” I gestured to the display behind me—and he walked over to look down at the assortment right beside us, lowering his voice to a whisper. “There could be some available. . . if you know the right person. . .”

“Eve, don't you just love this?” Eva's excited voice distracted me—and when I looked back to where the man had been standing just a moment ago, he was gone. . . searching for him, I found him at the front of the tent, speaking with another person. I turned to give Eva my attention. She was holding up a belt with the most beautiful markings I had ever seen for me to look over.

“I do. It's stunning.” I agreed, while running my fingers lightly over the markings on the belt. They felt smooth to the touch, but the slight bumps where each part of the pattern was, made it obvious that the design had somehow been etched into the leather. “But how could someone do this? It's so intricate.”

“I have no idea, but I'm definitely getting it.” With that, she went off toward the front of the store to speak to the man who must be the artist.

I continued to look at the weapon sheaths beside me, thinking about what he had said. . . and the way in which he had said it. Clearly, having a weapon was a very different prospect here. He had not said it was specifically allowed to own a weapon here—just as it had been in the caves—but his message had been clear. There were people in possession of weapons in the city. . . which made me begin to wonder just how different things were here.

So far, no one had gone over any rules or regulations with me. No one had told me what was or was not allowed. . . or how things worked on a day to day basis, aside from the woman in the dining hall who had said everyone pulled their weight.

The more I thought about how things might work here, the

more I realized that there must be considerably different rules. *Otherwise they are much more lax on the idea of punishment.* Thinking of that possibility made me wonder about things going on in the caves that I hadn't known about. *Could there have been people in the caves with weapons they should not have had?*

There were certainly a lot of things going on that the average person did not know about.

"Okay. This is so much better than just trading for something at stores. I probably gave less credits for this than I would have there. And this is so much better." Eva practically bounced back over to where I stood, obviously thrilled with her purchase. "Did you find anything you want?" She turned to look at the display beside me. "Oh! You should totally get this one." She picked up the beautifully etched quiver and arm guard that I had been looking at earlier. "It will look so great out there." I looked at the young woman in front of me and again found myself wondering about her. Nothing I had seen thus far in her personality accounted for what Astrid had told me. . . unless it was the other way around. Perhaps her roommates had been annoyed by the perky, cheerful, bouncy type. She nudged me playfully and lowered her voice to add, "You'd be the envy of all the other hunters."

Her words pulled me from my speculating. "Is that what I'll be doing as a job when the winter celebration is over? Did Astrid tell you?" I wondered why everyone was so sure that was what I would be doing when I was clear of this silly concussion. And why hadn't Astrid or Alexander said something about it? Was everyone just guessing—or had I just missed the obvious message?

"No." She shook her head, and then went on. "But it's kind of a no-brainer. You're a great hunter. They'd be silly to waste that." She turned back toward the front of the tent. "I'm going to go see what kind of deal I can get on this."

I started to speak up, but she waved away my objections before I could voice them. "You can always pay me back later if you insist." And then she rushed off again. I followed at a slower pace, curious to see just how she went about getting such a great price.

Of course, by the time I reached the pair of them, the deal had been completed and Eva turned to me with a triumphant grin. "Anything else you want to look at here?" I looked around for the man, but he had disappeared somewhere. Clearly I was not going to get any more answers now.

Shrugging a little, I smiled over at Eva. No need to ruin her excitement. "No. We can move on."

"Excellent. I tried yesterday, but there are so many of these stalls set up during the celebration, I just couldn't hit them all." She linked an arm through mine as we made our way to the next tent. We looked at art and rugs, shoes and dresses, scented soaps and little wooden toys. Eva didn't linger at all at the tent with toys. Even though there were plenty of other pieces of wood carvings—and even furniture—she rushed out of the tent without looking at another thing. I followed quickly, trying to decide if this was one of the things I should ask her about it or if it would be better to just keep my questions to myself.

Before I could think about it another moment, a surprisingly familiar squeal commanded my attention. Looking around for the source had me stifling a groan. Sandy and at least most of the kids she'd had in tow the day before were rushing toward me, nearly knocking people over in their mad dash forward through the marketplace.

"Oh! You're here! You're here! I wasn't certain you would be, but you're here!" She stopped suddenly and her hand flew up to cover her mouth for a moment before she started again in a somewhat muted voice. "Right. Concussion. I forgot. Sorry. I'm just so excited to see you again."

I nodded to her and the group behind her, uncertain what

exactly I was supposed to do—or say—to them. I certainly did not want to encourage her behavior, but at the same time, I wasn't certain there was anything I could have done to discourage it. I looked around for Eva, but she'd disappeared into another tent and I had no clue which one.

"Have you been down to lunch yet? The buffet is really great this year. They have all sorts of things you won't see again until next Winter. You really don't want to miss it. Hey, have you had a puff pastry yet? They are absolutely amazing! There's a booth right over here. I can show you." She started pulling me in the direction I had just come from and I started to tell her that I had already been treated to one, but she stopped suddenly. "Oh! Can you eat normal food yet?" She spun around on her heel, dropping my elbow in the process and I took the opportunity to step back a little.

"I can eat normal food now. I had a wonderful breakfast this morning and I have already had a puff pastry. Thank you. Yes, it was delicious."

She nodded furiously and was off again. "Where did you end up, in the stacks or the dorms? Is it just temporary? Because sometimes they put people in the dorms when they first arrive, but then they move them right away to the stacks. I've seen a couple of apartments in the stacks. They're nice. I hope to get there some day." The last word was said in a plaintive note and I scrambled to find something I could say that might be helpful. Fortunately, Eva walked up behind me and interrupted.

"Hi Sandy. I see you've met my new roommate. How are things?"

Sandy looked from me to Eva. . . and back to me several times, her mouth open slightly as if she was about to speak, but she said nothing.

Eva turned to look at the other kids who were with Sandy—who I had never even noticed moving out from behind us. "You guys enjoying the Winter Feast?" When she received nothing in return but heads slowly nodding, she went on. "Well, this is my first one, and Eve's first one so we're going to go explore some more. Great seeing you." And she pulled me backwards before any of them could say anything.

We were maybe twenty feet away when she turned a corner and we both started laughing. We laughed for a long time before we finally started to calm down. Eva was the first to speak. "Oh man. I don't believe I have ever seen her speechless. Even if the rest of the Feast is a total bore, that has made my day."

And before I could say anything, she was pulling me back

toward the tents. "Come on. There's still a lot to see. And we've got to go get lunch soon." I followed, vaguely aware of a hollow feeling in my stomach.

For the next half hour she moved from tent to tent, bargaining with people, trying on more clothes. . . and shoes, continuing to buy things the likes of which I had never seen before. I was amazed to watch her continue to amass things.

In the caves, we had only owned things that were absolutely essential. Even the dress and shoes she had shown me this morning were far more than the average person in the caves would have possessed. *Obviously she adapted quickly to the differences in how they do things here.*

I was also amazed that within minutes, Sandy and her group found us again. . . and again. Every tent we entered, she showed up again—no matter what direction we took or how far away from the last tent we wandered.

It must have begun to get on her nerves because the last time they showed up, Eva threw up her hands in frustration. "Oh man. I have had enough of this. Let's go eat."

Of course, we had no more than sat down at a table than she was there with at least a dozen other people. Eva had specifically chosen a table that only seated two—and in an area that was surrounded by already-full tables. It took no more than a few seconds for me to pick up on why. She had counted on Sandy showing up again and had figured that this at least would deter her.

"Eve, we just want to talk to you. . . ask you some questions." Sandy stood there, holding a small, narrow book in both hands. "Please."

"Sandy, could you just let us enjoy the Winter Feast? This is the first one for both of us." Eva's voice was surprisingly gentle, but when Sandy said nothing, she added, "Can't this wait. . . at least until the feast is over? I'm sure Eve would be happy to give you all the time you want then." She looked over at me and I nodded, unsure where precisely she was going with all of this, but happy to agree if it meant Sandy and her friends would stop dogging our heels at every turn.

Sandy didn't move though. She just stood there, staring, waiting, while Eva and I sat, unsure of what to do next.

At the tables around us, people were whispering, hands over their mouths as they spoke quietly, looking at the table we were sitting at—and the group of young people standing next to us with speculative glances.

"Sandy, we're making a scene. Could we please do this later?" Eva's voice was quieter, but much less friendly now.

And still. . . Sandy just stood there.

I looked at Eva—and she looked at me—and when, a moment later, several people pushed their way between the table and Sandy, we took advantage of the distraction and rushed away in the opposite direction.

TEN

Hope City

Year 45 A.E.

Day I74

Once we managed to escape Sandy and her ever-growing group again, we headed back to the marketplace, hoping we could perhaps find a way to get lost among the towering tents and crowds of people.

"If I didn't know better, I would think that girl has a tracking device on you." Eva laughed as she said it, but the comment reminded me of what Alexander had said the day before.

I had never known. . . never heard rumors or whispers of anything like that. . . even among the secrets Dad had shared with me. How was it possible that something like that could be so well hidden from the people? For that matter, what about the people who injected it to begin with. . . was there just one person—and how did they keep it from the parents? Had no parent ever asked for an explanation for the injection site? Beyond that. . . had no one ever stumbled across it accidentally or through injury? And, if not, how deep was it buried?

I had found no bandages on my body to give me any clue as to where they had removed it. And was there some chance they had inserted one of their own at the same time? *Would he have told me if they had?* I knew without asking that the answer would be no. He would certainly not have told me. It would have confirmed what I already suspected—that the city was no better than the caves in the ways that mattered.

They might have fancier clothes, and a feast that made the cave's meager celebrations look pitiful by comparison. . . and things might look better on the surface, but that did not mean that Alexander was any better than the Chancellor.

"Come on. I want to see if I can find the last piece for my costume." Eva headed for a tent off to the left and I followed, tucking my musings away—just as I had so often in the caves, keeping things that could be dangerous to myself. "I thought I would have time to finish it, but. . ." she shrugged as she walked into the tent.

I stopped a moment to look at the entrance Eva had just walked through without a second thought. There was something about it that was different from all the rest. It was dark and dingy, but in a way that almost looked as if it was on purpose. The tent itself was a dark brown—and made of a much coarser material than the others. It was held up by metal poles like the others, but each one was different—and they looked as if they'd been salvaged from a trash heap; dirty, with flaking and chipped paint, rust spots and grease all over.

Careful to avoid brushing up against anything, I followed Eva inside—and saw immediately that it was no different. Items were set up on broken doors and bent metal siding, piled into rusty buckets and old, worn wood barrels. The items themselves were a curiosity as well; metal goggles and strange hats, clothing made of metal and leather and looking more like it belonged on a machine than a person.

"Isn't it great! They have some of the best stuff!" Eva's voice was full of excitement as she perused each table and barrel. "Oh! I love these!" She held up a pair of rusty goggles to me, dropping them in my hand when I lifted it reluctantly.

I looked down at the greasy, rusty, dingy goggles in my hand and tried to figure out why anyone would get so excited over them. There was absolutely nothing special I could see about them, and it made even less sense when I thought about the dress she had been so excited about finding in the box of clothes they had left for me.

I turned to set the goggles back down on the table next to me, but then it occurred to me that Eva might actually want them. . . given the fuss she'd made over them. . . so I carried them along with me when she moved deeper into the tent and I followed. I wove my way through, slowly following Eva's meandering path, working hard to avoid rough edges and greasy-looking stains—all the while thinking to myself that the dim lighting inside the dark tent was not very helpful at all.

By the time I reached Eva, she was deep in discussion with someone whom I presumed was the proprietor. They were discussing hats and goggles and whether or not someone named Nicolas would be able to top his costume from the year before. I half listened as I looked around aimlessly, still somewhat curious as to what it was about such things that had Eva so excited.

I had just about given up hope of finding a reason, when I spotted a display behind the woman Eva was talking to. It was turned slightly away from me, but something about the arrangement of feathers and shiny silver pieces caught my attention and I wound my way over to it to get a closer look.

As I moved around tables between me and the display, I began to see that it was some sort of outfit, put together on a human form to show off how it could look on a person. I could even see the blank face on a head peeking out from under the elaborate, feathered mask—and the closer I got to it, the more I liked what I was seeing. When I moved around from beside the wide circle of tables surrounding the display, I was even more intrigued by the full costume.

"Find something you like?" Eva's voice startled me and I jumped a little. "Yes." I answered, still a little surprised myself.

"You should get it. Wear it tomorrow. You'll be a hit." The excitement in her voice was infectious. I found myself thinking about how I might look if the pieces were on me instead of the faceless form in front of us.

"I thought I was supposed to wear that dress you pulled out of the box." She waved my words away. "You wear the dress to dinner. This is for the day. Everyone wears an elaborate costume during the early festivities." The enthusiasm in her voice had me looking longingly at the costume again. "I've been putting mine together for weeks and I just found the finishing touches. It's going to be great!"

"Does that mean all of the things in this tent are parts of a costume?" I still could not understand why anyone would purposely wear something that looked dirty or rusty on purpose, but I wondered then—if it was a costume—if the rust or dirt was real or perhaps if it was painted on somehow. I held up the goggles I still held and looked at them much more carefully.

On closer inspection, I could see that the rust was painted on —and when I rubbed a finger carefully over the greasy area, it was also fake.

"Yes. All of the things in this tent—and probably several others—are props, fake, costume pieces. There may be only one Winter Feast, but they have several other events where everyone dresses in costume." She lowered her voice before adding, "There's not a lot to do underground you know."

I couldn't help myself. I laughed. "Don't I know it."

And then she was laughing with me. "You know, sometimes it's hard to remember all that time in the caves. Life here is just so different." There was something in her voice. . . she sounded wistful, but also somehow resigned—and I thought back to our conversation in the middle of the night. She had left someone behind and it was probably killing her every day.

It certainly was me. Every time I thought of Jude. . . and my mother and grandparents, I wanted to cry—which was why I ruthlessly forced those thoughts out of my mind whenever it happened.

“So, are you gonna get it? It really would be stunning on you.”

Somehow. . . between the excitement in her voice and the enchanting look of the ensemble and the determination to distract myself , I found myself agreeing. “Okay. How do I do it? You said I have starter credits. . . are they in that box? Should I have brought them with me?”

She only laughed. “No. They're linked to your code. Come on —I'll show you.” And she pulled me back toward the woman she'd been talking to earlier. “She wants the display costume, Lil.”

“Excellent choice.” And the woman Eva had called Lil looked me over carefully for several long seconds before responding. “And, as luck would have it, I think it's just her size.”

“Perfect.” Eva clapped her hands together. “And I'll take these, along with the hat we discussed.” She lay several things down on the small table between us before turning to me. “Do you still have those goggles, Eve?” In answer, I held them up, though my attention had wandered back to the costume. Thinking of the unwanted attention I'd been getting from Sandy and her group, I was beginning to wonder if it wouldn't be better to find something a bit less eye-catching.

"Eve, you want to see this." Her fingers closed around my arm gently; that and her words pulled my attention back to her as she went through the motions of the trade. Lil was holding a little box over Eva's arm and when I looked closer, I could see that there was a strange purple light coming from the box—and in that light I could see a pattern marked on Eva's wrist. The light disappeared too quickly for me to get a really good look at the design, but there had been numbers and patterns all mixed together in a square of sorts. After a moment, Lil nodded and I saw then that she was looking at a screen of the same sort our master-at-arms in the caves had used when she'd checked out hunting equipment to us. *This place is just full of surprises.*

A moment later, Lil turned to me with a smile. "Anything else beside the fairy costume?"

I looked around the store, but since I hadn't really looked at anything seriously before the costume had caught my attention, I didn't really have an answer. Turning to Eve, I said as much. "I don't really know. Should I look around a bit more?"

"Couldn't hurt. You'll hold the costume for her, won't you Lil?" The shopkeeper nodded and Eva pulled me back into the store, starting with the things on the tables around the costume Lil had called a fairy. I forced my attention to the objects around it with a new objectivity. There were items on the table that were definitely meant to go with the costume; tight leggings with a feathery pattern, bracelets made of metal pieces that were intricately woven into a vine pattern, gloves with feathers attached in an arrangement that gave them the look of a flower, more goggles—though these were shinier and covered in vines and flowers and more feathers.

"Eva, what's the appeal of the goggles?" I turned to her, holding the pair up to her.

"Oh. These are nice ones." She looked up at the costume beside us. "I'm not sure you'd want to trade these for the mask. . . or have a full hat either. . . Maybe a Lolita hat."

Before I could ask what she was talking about, Lil appeared beside her, holding up a rounded band with a small hat on top; feathers sticking up in a plume alongside it, silvery vines woven around the brim like a band, and a smattering of glittering silver all over. "You could easily wear the goggles with this." And she slid them onto my face, stopping short of slipping them over my eyes; moving them up on top of my head. Then she settled the band over my head behind them, sliding the band itself behind my ears and then turning to fasten a closure of some sort that I hadn't even seen attached to the band under my low ponytail.

Then she pulled and tugged on my hair for a few seconds. I started to protest until I realized it only felt like she was pulling the ponytail out. She must have achieved the desire effect because she turned and pulled down the mask—and then she put a hand at my back and turned me toward the front of the tent until I was looking at a standing mirror I hadn't noticed before.

My reflection was nearly a shock. Whatever she'd done to my hair made it look fuller and puffed up behind the hat and goggles—which gave me a much more intriguing look than I could have expected. A moment later, she walked around to settle the mask on my face and then moved away so I could see —and I was shocked again.

My earlier worries about going with something less eye-catching faded away. I might get people's attention in this costume, but there was very little chance that Sandy or her friends would recognize me in this. I didn't even recognize myself in it. . . and I felt Eva's earlier excitement filling me as well. *No wonder they like to dress in costume. It's intoxicating.*

"I'll take these too." I heard myself saying—and marveled again at the difference the mask made in my voice. It was another boon. Sandy likely wouldn't recognize my voice either. "Is there anything else I should add to it?" I turned to look back at Lil and Eva, who was wearing a very smug expression indeed.

Lil said nothing, just moved back to the table and selected several small items.

Finding a seat in the dining hall for dinner proved nearly impossible when we were finally able to tear ourselves away from Sandy and her rapidly growing mob of teens. How they managed to consistently find me was a puzzle I was not certain I wanted to know the answer to, but every time we had managed to get away from her group today, they had found us within an hour.

It was getting exhausting.

"Here's hoping we can eat in peace." Eva tapped her glass against mine and then took a drink, so I followed suit. The drink was unexpectedly flavorful—and unlike anything I had tasted before. I turned to my new roommate. She might only have been here three months, but she certainly seemed to know more about this place than I would have expected. "Eva, what is this?"

She looked over at me. . . and then at the glass I was holding up, before she answered. "It's wine. Haven't you. . . No, right. You wouldn't have. You were in the family corridor." She shook her head a little and then went on. "You might want to stick with a single glass if this is the first you've ever had."

"I only have the one glass." I insisted.

"Yes, but they will bring around bottles in a bit and offer refills. They may even have several different ones you could try, but I don't suggest it if you've never had any before. . . especially with a concussion."

"Why?" She wasn't exactly answering my question.

"Wine is alcohol. In small doses, it's fine, but when you're not used to it, it can be bad."

"Especially when I have a concussion, right? But why?" It felt like there was still something missing from her explanation, but I wasn't sure how to ask without knowing what.

"The easiest way to explain it is to say that alcohol does something to you when you drink a lot of it—and every person is different in what a lot is to them. Some people can only handle a glass or two. Some people could drink a whole bottle. . . not that anyone down here gets that chance much."

She laughed a little before going on. "It's not going to hurt you. It's just something you want to be careful about the first time you have it. If it's too much for you, the most a glass will do is make your brain a bit fuzzy. No big deal." She shrugged the consequences away, but I had already pushed my glass aside. No matter how interesting the taste, I wasn't sure I wanted to chance something odd happening to me.

"Can I get something else to drink?"

She laughed again before answering. "Yes, they'll have other kinds of drinks when they come around with the bottles. Plenty of people stick to just the one glass so they have to have other options on hand." She watched me until I nodded and then applied herself to her food, so I did the same.

With nothing else to drink, I was overly cautious to cut up everything into tiny little pieces before I put the first bite in my mouth. I was not taking any chances. And, even though she had said they would bring more drinks around, there was no one I could see moving around, carrying drinks of any kind so I let caution rein.

Very quickly I discovered that taking small bites was a good thing for more reasons than one. I was able to savor each bite —and enjoy the truly exquisite food that was so much more fancy and delicious than anything I had ever tasted in the caves. . . even at a celebration.

Halfway through the meal, someone did appear at my elbow with a bottle and offered to refill my glass. . . or they started to anyway, until they saw that my glass was still mostly full. “What else would you prefer, miss?”

I asked several questions about the different drinks available before settling on something called hot cocoa and he suggested I take a careful sip to be certain it was to my liking so I lifted the mug to my lips and—since I could feel how warm the cup felt in my hand—I did as he suggested and took a careful sip.

He must have seen from the expression on my face that I was enjoying the drink because when I turned to offer my unwanted glass of wine to him, he had already moved on to the next person. I tried to get his attention, but most of the people beside me were apparently happy with their wine because he was nearly the length of the end of the table already. With a shrug, I set the cup back down and kept eating.

Surprisingly, the rest of dinner was relatively uneventful. Eva and I ate, talking a bit about how tonight's food compared with the typical dinner food, which I had yet to see. Eva was quick to remind me that she had only been in the city for the past three months, but the food was better than anything served in the caves.

Eventually someone took away my wine glass, which I was grateful for since the two sips I had taken had done precisely what Eva had warned me they would do; make my brain fuzzy. Everything in the room had a slightly blurry outline and I felt strangely warm—though that could have had something to do with the hot cocoa.

Sometime later, when nearly half the dining hall had emptied, there was a ruckus by the large entryway—and though it was impossible to truly know what happened first—the screams of the excited teens or the ones of the poor boy who was trampled beneath the mob of rushing feet—I was immediately reminded of the marketplace and the group who had been so much in a rush, they had nearly knocked several people over as they moved forward so quickly.

The next thing I knew, Eva was pulling me up and away from the table. Then she was pushing me towards the opposite end of the room. The crowd followed, and I was grateful that the dining hall was at least half empty. However, I did have a moment to wonder if the crowd could have gathered such momentum if there had been more people in the cavernous room.

Only seconds before the crowd caught up to us, Eva pulled me through a door and and into a mostly dark tunnel. She stopped just long enough to throw a lever that must have been a lock of some sort before turning and moving down the tunnel. I followed her, not wanting to be left where I would only end up lost.

"I cannot believe she did that. What was that girl thinking?"

"Who?" I asked, but I was pretty sure I knew who she meant.

"Sandy. Who else?" Her voice was full of an emotion I was hesitant to identify. It sounded much stronger than simple annoyance—and I started to think that she might be over-reacting a bit, but then I thought of the screams of at least one person who had been caught under the rushing feet of a careless crowd and I realized she was right to react so strongly.

"What do we do now?" I asked—then waited for an answer. . . and waited. . . as she turned to the right, and then the left, and then right again, hoping she knew where she was going in the inky darkness.

ELEVEN

Hope City

Year 45 A.E.

Day I75

The last day of the Winter Feast was more fantastic. . . and more nerve-wracking. . . than anything I had ever experienced. Everyone, everywhere, was dressed either in fancy clothes or in a costume of some sort. When I passed a large group of people, I had a moment to be glad Eva had walked into that tent yesterday—and that I had spotted this costume. It was proving to be a perfect choice.

Walking the halls with a mask over my apparently famous face and an elaborate costume that easily hid some aspects of my build, while enhancing others, and in ways that I never had before, made me feel almost like a different person—not to mention the way my voice sounded different—and, after the debacle of the evening before, I was glad for the anonymity. Sandy might mean well, but several people had been hurt in the crowd and there was less and less possibility of my blending in and going unnoticed anywhere in the city now, either by Sandy and her group or by the people who had been between me and them at dinner.

As I moved along the catwalk floors above and then the rock floor below, where the makeshift marketplace had been the day before, I noticed that nearly everyone I walked past watched my progress and, for a moment I was overcome with nerves. It hadn't been my intention to attract a lot of attention.

Fortunately, I quickly realized that I was not the only one to draw so many eyes. There were elaborate costumes all over—and most everyone stared as each person went by, so evidently this was just part of the experience.

Going on memory alone, I made my way to the dining hall, watching for Eva as I went. She had been gone already when I woke up. . . no note or anything. I presumed she had just wanted to get an early start in showing off her own costume, so I had put mine on, using the mirror on the back of the bathroom door to help.

Since Eva had said breakfast would be a big deal this last

morning of the feast, I didn't want to take a chance on missing it. I felt certain that was part of the reason she'd been up and gone so early.

As I moved across the room, I tried to keep a close watch for the hat she would be wearing; the elaborate design that she had apparently ordered before I even took notice of my costume. It was surprising how many people walked by me with a similar look, but not one of them was Eva—and no one had a hat quite like hers either.

It was frustrating.

When I reached the dining hall—with no sign of her, and no long lines in front of me, I decided I had better go ahead and get breakfast. I filled a plate with as much as I could fit on it and turned to find a seat, bumping solidly into Sandy.

"I'm so sorry."

Forcing myself to take a deep breath, I tried to get control over my suddenly chaotic thoughts. What was it about this young woman that rubbed me the wrong way—other than her penchant for stirring up trouble. "Sorry for what?" I spoke without thinking, without remembering that I was safe behind an elaborate mask. . . And when her eyes widened in recognition, I wanted to scream in frustration. Why had I let my mouth get the better of me?

With the damage already done, I went on. “Sorry for dogging my steps since I arrived, sorry for chasing me down with a mob, or sorry about that young man who was trampled under the feet of your followers last night?”

For a moment. . . just one moment. . . I almost wondered if I had been too harsh, but then I reminded myself of the young man in the medical wing, being treated for broken bones, bruises and physiological distress. And at least Sandy had the good sense to look ashamed. “All of it. I'm sorry for all of it. I don't know what has gotten into me the last few days.” She kept shifting her weight back and forth from one foot to the other and twisting her hands together in front of her. “I'm not like this. . . really. You can ask any of my friends. They'll tell you.”

“There's a problem with that, Sandy—and you know exactly what it is, too. You've made all of your friends just as nuts over me as you are. I'm not sure it would help to speak to any of them.”

She looked down at the floor as she answered this time, refusing to meet my eyes. “You're right. . . again, I'm so sorry. I promise to stop—and I promise to ask the rest of them to stop. And we will do whatever sort of penance you think we deserve to make it up to you.”

I stopped her right there. "That's just it, Sandy. It's not me you have to make it up to. You have to do whatever you can do to make it up to anyone who was hurt in all that crazy mess. And you need to go and see if there's any cleaning up you need to do as well." I looked around me at the dining hall, but it was immediately obvious that any mess from the evening before had already been taken care of—which made me wonder. . . were there still people who worked during the Winter Feast?

Of course there are. I felt like smacking myself when I realized that I already knew the answer to that. There would have to be. Otherwise, how would the food get cooked? Who would clean up after the meals? I started to ask Sandy about it, but she was busy answering my earlier statement.

"You are exactly right, and that is exactly what we will do." And she turned then, rushing off without another word.

With no one else nearby, I started toward a table at the back of the room, just as my head began to pound—a painful reminder of precisely why I had no job assigned to me yet. Taking a deep breath, I walked over to the table and felt a bit of relief when I sat down to eat.

Eva's descriptions of the morning meal for today had been such that I'd been certain she had to be exaggerating. I'd almost been expecting to be disappointed, but there was nothing on the plate in front of me or in the food available this morning that could have left anyone wanting. Though I had tried to go easy with my selections, I had piled my plate high.

"Hey! You started without me. . ." Eva dropped onto the seat next to me with a huff—and I turned to look at her, expecting to see the fantastic costume and enormous hat. . . but she was wearing a plain grey jumpsuit.

I stared at her for several long seconds, watching her hand as she reached over and took a piece of bacon off my tray. . . and finally the words found their way out. "Where's your costume?"

"My. . ." She broke the bacon in half and popped one piece in her mouth, looking at the food on other trays as people walked by our table. "That looks good. I have to get some of that." She turned back to me. "You didn't get any donuts?"

"I did. . . I think." I waved a hand absently at my tray, with three plates piled higher than I would normally be comfortable with—had it not been for every other person carrying as much or more on their own trays. I knew I wouldn't be able to eat it all, but I could take most of it with me to snack on later. "They're somewhere. . ."

"Oh. . . Okay. I won't take yours. I was going to say I'll get you some when I go for my own tray." She popped the other piece of bacon in her mouth. "This is great. They don't have bacon very often. I'll get you some more." And with that, she started to stand.

"Eva, where have you been?"

"Huh?" She had pushed herself up from the table and already half-turned toward the doors leading to the buffet, but she spun back around at my question. "I was at my post. . . in communications."

"But I thought. . ." I shook my head a little before starting again. "I thought you said no one worked during the feast." Even as I was saying it, I realized it made no sense. Of course, everyone worked during the feast. They probably just had lighter shifts or something.

"No, silly. . . everyone still works. Some of us get lighter workloads and some of us get up extra early to get our shift out of the way in time to get to the fun." She waved a hand dismissively. "Speaking of which, I'd better get some breakfast before it's all gone. I'll be back." And she rushed off then, giving me no further chance to argue or question.

Seeing the evidence right in front of me, I suddenly felt foolish. It was silly of me to think no one worked just because it was a special holiday celebration. Things still had to be done. There was cooking and cleaning and surveillance to do —and someone would still have to do it.

Boy, this concussion is a doozy. . . to have my thinking so off.

Of course, there was also a good chance it was just that there was so much to take in. Clearly I had arrived at the worst possible time—and things would likely only get more complicated once the celebration ended and it was time for me to take my own place among the city workers. . . whatever that might be.

Less than ten minutes passed before Eva dropped an even more heavily laden tray beside mine. She settled onto the seat next to me again and immediately started piling things on my tray, where I had begun to make a dent in the enormous piles of food.

"Eva, I can't possibly eat all of this."

"Nonsense. You'll get through it. . . eventually." She put two white boxes on top of the table in front of our trays. "Whatever you can't eat now, put in there and we'll take it back with us when I go change." She looked over at me then, adding, "or, when I go change anyway. You don't have to go back with me." Then, without another word, she dug into the food in front of her.

"I'm fine going back with you. I just wasn't thinking this

morning." I laughed before going on, "I was just remembering what you said yesterday—and I was certain you'd already left so you wouldn't take a chance on missing breakfast. I rushed off trying to catch up with you."

Eva laughed and then dug into her food again. I ate much more slowly, savoring the delightful tastes of foods I had never even seen before—and the ones I had only ever had once or perhaps twice in the caves.

At least the box I could understand. . . saving food was something we were all taught early—that, and not wasting anything. Putting the leftover food into the box Eva had set in front of me was like second nature, though after I did, I still felt silly trying to finish what I had left on my plate. It was all too much.

Will I ever get used to the way things are here? The longer I was here, the less I thought I might, but it wasn't like I had anywhere else to go. *One way or another, I guess I'll have to adapt.*

By the time Eva began filling her own box with the few extras left on her tray, I was beginning to regret eating as much as I had. My stomach was more full than it had ever been before that I could remember—and much of it overly-sweet for first thing in the morning.

Feeling more than a little nauseous, I followed Eva without a word back to our apartment, where I proceeded to strip off as much of my costume as possible on my way to collapse on my narrow bed.

And. . . either I dozed off or Eva was just ridiculously quiet—because the next thing I knew, she was popping her head in through my open door. "What do you say, Eve, you ready to get back out there and have some fun?"

Part of me wanted to ignore her. Part of me wanted to find the energy to get up. . . just so I could go shut the door in her face. But part of me also wanted the chance to get up and go explore all of the things that were supposed to be so great about this day, this last day of the biggest celebration I would likely see all year. Eva was not the only one who had told me the third day of this Winter Feast was proclaimed to be the most amazing celebration the city saw all year—and I knew, deep down, that I shouldn't miss it.

But there was also a part of me—the part that had yet to get used to any of the ways of these city people. . . and secretly thought I never would—who wanted to just stay here in the safety of my room, far away from any craziness, far from rabid fans who had already found me today—even in costume, far from all of the things that were strange and foreign to me and likely always would be.

"Come on Eve, you really don't want to miss this. It won't come around for an entire year. That's a lot of days to wait for something." Eva walked over to the bed and nudged me gently. "I promise, it'll be worth it." When that didn't work, she tried again. "I promise you'll feel better once you start moving around and your body has a chance to start digesting all of that food." When I still didn't move, she walked around to stand right in front of me. "You will not feel better just lying there. And, you'll miss everything. And I promise that you will regret it if you just lie there and miss all of the activities today."

She walked toward the door. "And I'm not missing them, either. I've been waiting for months."

I wasn't certain if she had simply walked out of the room or if she was already heading for the front door, but I could hear her footsteps in the hall and, as timid as I felt about dealing with the circus that certainly waited on the outside of our apartment, I knew she was right.

I would regret it if I missed everything. And I knew she was right about the rest, too. So I did what she wanted. I pushed myself off the bed, gathered up the discarded pieces of my costume and headed for the hall.

"I knew you couldn't resist." Her smug smile gave me pause for just a moment, but I reigned in my annoyance and pulled my costume back together.

After only a few seconds, Eva walked over to help and together we managed to get it all back into place rather quickly.

And then we were walking out the door together and into a much noisier hallway than we had left only a few minutes before. *Unless I did fall asleep. . .* unfortunately, I had not thought to look at the digital in the apartment. My wrist digital had never been returned to me, and the volume all around us made it impractical to even try to ask Eva if she knew what time it was.

I could only hope that we would walk past a clock at some point soon enough for me to figure it out. *Not that it matters at this point.*

I followed Eva along the catwalk-like hallway, concentrating on keeping sight of her in the sea of bodies that had appeared since our return from breakfast. Somehow she wound her way through everyone—almost as if she had been here all the time, and never even lived in the caves. *And she has only been here three months.*

It was difficult to think of, but it worried me that in only three months, I would be as acclimated as Eva, where the things about the city that were so markedly different would feel perfectly normal to me. Would I forget my parents' value so quickly. . . or Jude's?

As the all-too familiar pain clutched at my heart, I found myself wondering if there was a chance that Eva had begun to throw herself into the happenings around her to try and distract herself from that pain in her own heart. She had lost her love. . . she had as much as said it that first night, speaking of how long it had been since she had been separated from her own mysterious *amour.*

Looking around at the crowd of bodies, at the blatantly sensual displays that I had never witnessed in the caves, thinking of the extravagant clothing and costumes and food everyone here was surrounded by, I was certain that was at least a part of it.

Either she had thrown herself into the lifestyle here—or she had been just as overwhelmed by it all as I had been and somehow had succumbed to it over time. Either way, it was not at all comforting to me—not one bit.

"Come on, Eve. Let's go have some fun!" Eva pulled me with her, and with little choice to do otherwise, I pushed through the crowd with her. From our level—eighteen floors above the ground—we could see the area where the marketplace had stood just the day before. It was filled with people, but no tents that I could see.

I wondered what was in store for the day's events, but could never have hoped to be heard above the massive swell of noise all around us, so I didn't waste my breath. . . I just followed Eva.

TWELVE

Hope City

Year 45 A.E.

Day I75

By the time we made it to the lower levels, I was beginning to notice that I felt hungry again—which turned out to be fortuitous since discovering that I had fallen asleep and stayed that way for more than an hour, apparently not even being woken up by Eva leaving the apartment. . . and later coming back to get me. Since it had taken another hour after that to put my costume back together, get out the door, and make our way here, lunch was already being served when we entered the dining hall.

"They work shorter shifts today too, but there's still plenty of good stuff." Eva stepped into the long line and I followed. "As long as we get to it in time." She nudged my shoulder and laughed, motioning to the length of the line ahead of us. Looking at it I could see that it would likely be another half hour before we actually made it to the front of the line.

While waiting, Eva chattered on about her morning with me. . . and with the two young men in front of us. It sounded to me like she'd had a very busy morning, but she shrugged it off as though it was nothing by comparison to some of the other professions in the city. . . or perhaps to any normal working day.

"So, you like your job here?" I asked her later, as we made our way to a table. "Is it the same as what you did in the caves or something different?"

"It's the same thing I did in the caves. . . or the same thing I would have done." She shrugged again before going on. "I had finished with my training, but I never got a chance to really get started." She looked up at me, an odd expression on her face. "I would have liked to get my hands on those communications. . . I mean, really get my hands on them." She took a bite, but added a moment later, "There was something going on there. I don't know what. . . but something."

Something about the way she said it reminded me of all the things my dad had told me when I was younger—about the way certain communications were funneled only through specific people. Even though he had been in a position of some significance on the Chancellor's staff, there were a lot of things he was not allowed to see or hear—or even to know about.

I had always wondered if he'd found out something he was not supposed to know, but was perhaps afraid to tell us about it. If he had, it was one secret he had never shared.

With that in mind, I pressed on, hoping Eva might have some reason for what had happened that night all those months ago—even if she didn't know it. "What makes you think there was something going on?"

She didn't even hesitate.

"Oh, lots of reasons. There were rooms filled with sophisticated equipment that we weren't even allowed in. They tried to tell us it had something to do with the delicacy of the machines and that only select personnel were ever trained on it, but that's bull. The equipment we worked on was plenty sturdy." She waved a hand in dismissal as she went on. "And from what I know about the mechanics and such, more sophisticated machines would not only have been more sturdy, they would have been newer than what we had—so there would have been a lot less worry over something happening to them."

I started to speak up, but she kept going. . . so I kept listening.

"Not that it would have mattered. With no one else to listen to, why would you need more sophisticated equipment anyway? I think there was something entirely different going on in those rooms. They just didn't want us to know about it." She nodded when she finished and I waited several long seconds before I spoke again.

"Didn't I hear somewhere though that there was a base on our moon where they sent the most important leadership of the planet before that rogue moon hit us?"

She nodded. "There was, but we were told there was some sort of accident about thirty years ago, before they could bring them all back down." She stopped there, took a bite, but before she had even finished chewing, she looked over at me with an odd expression. "But you know, if somehow they were wrong—and the leadership survived, you can bet that they don't know we survived. If they had, we wouldn't be answering to that Chancellor."

She turned her attention back to her food.

I thought about what she said. "Well, at least the people in the caves wouldn't be. We don't have to worry about him anymore, or do we?"

Her eyes widened at that. "What do you mean by that, Eve? What do you know?"

I spoke carefully, keeping my suspicions to myself, working hard to keep an innocent expression on my face when I answered. "I only mean that he's there and we're here and Alexander's in charge over here. . . right?"

"Right." She answered—a little too quickly, it seemed—and then turned back to her food.

Inside I was celebrating. I had known all along that there was more going on here than anyone could see on the surface. There was something not quite right about the whole place. *Looks like Alexander is no better than the Chancellor. . . that is, unless he's under the Chancellor's control. I guess he could just be a weak, pathetic pawn.*

I ate slowly, thinking over what Eva had said—and what she had implied without actually saying anything. . . and what she hadn't meant to draw attention to.

There was definitely more going on down here than anyone was saying.

I will have to be careful or I might just end up in more trouble than I can handle. Suddenly I was very glad for the self-defense moves my grandfather had taught me. . . and for the excellent hand-to-hand combat training we had all received in the hunter's class. *It just might prove useful here as well.*

The thought was both comforting and frightening.

When we finished lunch and headed back out to the great room at the base of the stacks, Eva walked slightly ahead of me, looking back every few minutes, always smiling widely. Yet she had not said a word to me since she'd last answered me in the dining hall before turning every ounce of her attention to finishing her food.

I knew I had hit a nerve somewhere. . . somehow. Although she obviously had no qualms about sharing her own suspicions about things not being quite how they should be in the caves, she had closed her mouth tighter than the huge gates when I had gotten too close to something troubling about the way things were in the city.

And I couldn't decide if that meant she knew something about what it was that I suspected, or if it meant she was just overly protective of the people who had rescued her and couldn't stand the idea of anyone suspecting them of something nefarious.

Not that it matters. I'm not going to win any friends making accusations—and if they are hiding something and she knows about it, she's not going to tell me. If only I had an 'in' somewhere in the city. . . someone who knows the score—or at least someone who knows how to find things out. It was at that moment that my mind summoned up the face of the one person I had been avoiding up to now. She was in surveillance. She might have some way to find out things, *but could I endanger her by asking? Would it be a danger to ask? If they watch people here like they watch them in the caves. . .* I realized she would know that, too. And I figured it was a safe bet that she would know if there was a place we could talk where no one could see—or hear.

Moving through the crowd, I made a point to look out for the young woman whom I was certain would do just about anything—if it meant spending time with me.

Any questions I had about the rules here in the city being

different were answered by the behavior of the people all around us as we made our way through the crowds throughout the afternoon. Everyone was drinking what looked like the wine Eva had introduced me to at dinner the night before—wine that I had seen being passed around again at lunch today.

Watching the behavior exhibited by nearly every person we moved past made me glad I had taken no more than a couple of sips the evening before—and that I had ignored it completely at lunch today. There might be no way to know for certain whether one led to the other, but I had enough of a suspicion that the behavior must be in some way connected to the alcohol, that I was happy to steer clear of it all.

I certainly don't want to learn to enjoy something that would cause me to behave in such a manner.

"Some of these people are going to have such a headache tomorrow." Eva said as she watched a particularly rowdy young man who was hanging upside down from a pole that stuck out from the upper level catwalk, pitching her voice above the nearly unbearable level of noise coming from every direction around us. "They're getting an early start, that's for sure."

It was obvious she had either forgotten that she was worried about speaking to me or she had decided to let it go and get back to where we had been before I asked the unfortunate question. Secretly I hoped it was the latter. Perhaps she would even forget about it if I stopped asking her any questions that might remind her of my suspicions.

"Especially if he falls." Was all I said in return, laughing with her at his crazy antics. I hoped it was the alcohol that was causing him to behave so. If it wasn't, I didn't want to think of the reasons behind it.

"Nah, he's pretty toasted. Even if he falls, he's so out of it, he won't feel a thing—and I seriously doubt he'll even remember any of it. That headache will be alcohol induced for sure." She laughed and then moved on when he did indeed fall.

I watched for a moment, trying to decide if there was something I could do to help—and wondering why no one around him was helping—when he stood, reached out to one of the people nearby and took the cup they handed him, tipping the cup up to drain it so quickly he couldn't possibly have tasted whatever was in it.

When he laughed and moved off to follow the people who were forming some sort of crazy line of shouting, gyrating bodies, I shook my head a little at the strangeness of it all and then turned to follow Eva.

It took me several minutes to find her in the crowd. There

were just too many bodies, too many costumes, too much noise—and I found myself wanting to go and lie down again—which was what I told her when I finally did find her.

Fortunately, she agreed that my concussion was likely not up to the noise level. "The big party tonight is going to be even worse. You won't want to stay around for any of that." She looked around at the crowd as we made our way to the first level. "I admit this is even a bit much for me. I mean, people have been telling me about the Winter Feast for weeks, but I had no idea it was like this."

I was already nodding with her. "We could both go up. It's not as if anyone is going to miss us."

She looked at me—and there was something in her expression that made me certain that she had not forgotten about our conversation at lunch. "I think I'm gonna stay awhile. Maybe I'll go check out some of the other areas. Maybe one of them is quieter. The stacks is tricky because it's so big, you think it could never get this loud, but the noise just bounces off everything and multiplies."

"Yeah." I agreed absently, still trying to work out how to get past that blasted slip-up.

"But you go get some rest. I'll come up and get you for dinner later. You won't want to miss the last feast."

Seeing that I was not going to win, I agreed. "That sounds great. I'll just go rest."

"Yes, do. And get out of your costume. You'll want to wear your dress to dinner tonight." She was squeezing my hands now, her voice filled with excitement. "Maybe I'll come up a bit early. You don't have any yet, but we have a similar enough skin tone, you could use some of my makeup." Her excitement was spilling over onto me now. I had no idea what she was talking about, but I found myself looking forward to it.

"Yeah," was all I could manage, lost as I was.

"Great. Okay. You go rest and I'll be up in a while." And she was off, dancing in the bouncy, twitchy way everyone else was, blending into the crowd immediately.

Once in our small apartment, I began pulling off pieces of my costume, grateful for release from the heavy, hard, sticky things. When I had freed myself from every piece, I took the time for a long, hot shower. One thing I was grateful for here was the water. . . and the pressure, too. The water beat down on my sore and abused muscles—muscles that ached much more now that I was alone and there was nothing else to distract me.

After I showered, I pulled on the least fancy clothes from the box and wandered into the living area, pulling a book off the shelf that had caught my attention earlier. I dropped into one of the big, soft, over-stuffed chairs and settled down into the squishy material that felt exactly like a soft pillow. But I never even opened the book. . .

The next thing I knew, Eva was shaking me awake. She was wrapped in a towel and her hair was hanging loosely down her back, obviously wet. "Come on. I let you sleep while I took my shower, but we've got to get ready now or we're going to be late." She turned and headed for her bedroom and I took a moment to stretch before following.

This place is making me lazy. I had slept most of the day away. I had slept ridiculously late the day before—and no one had ever told me how long I had been unconscious in the infirmary—or wherever it was that I had been before they woke me and took me to Alexander.

When I walked into Eva's room, her dress was laid out over her bed in a waterfall of shimmering red. As I moved closer, I could see the light reflecting off little, glittering clear stones that were sewn onto the dress at irregular intervals. When I reached the bed and looked down at it, I was glad to remember the dress she had pulled out for me was more modest, much less daring, and much less of an obvious attention grabber.

As if the red was not enough to grab everyone's attention, the neckline was so low I wondered how Eva thought she was going to walk, dance. . . or pretty much anything, without showing off her feminine assets—as my grandmother had called them—to everyone. To top that off, there were no sleeves, just tiny little straps that went over the shoulders. Moving closer, I noticed that there were several long slits in the full-length, attached skirt that would come dangerously close to showing off what little the top of the dress did not.

I swallowed hard when I thought about my own dress. Had I paid enough attention to it? What if it were just as risque as Eva's? With that in mind, I tripped a little over my own feet as I rushed out of her room, down the hall, and into my own—where Eva stood, removing my dress from the closet.

"We forgot to steam it, but it actually looks like most of the wrinkles have hung out already."

I ignored the comment and moved to take the hanger from her, turning the dress around and around, looking at it from different angles while holding it away from me, but up high enough that I could judge how it would fit to my body—where it would show off parts of me that were usually hidden under bulky clothing, and trying to decide if I had enough courage to go outside. . . to mingle with people. . . in a dress that was actually much less conservative than I had initially thought.

"Eva, I'm not sure I can do this. Can I just go like this? Or better yet, couldn't I just stay in? I don't really care about the special food. I'm perfectly content to stay here and eat whatever." I turned to the small desk that sat in the corner, lifting the small pack I had been handed that first night out of the chair. "I still have several of these packets they made up for me to eat that first night, too. I never did get around to eating them because I fell asleep... and then I was sick..." I trailed off, feeling slightly nauseous at the reminder—or maybe it was the thought of going anywhere in that dress.

"No way, Eve. You can't miss this. It won't come around for a year. That is a lot of days to wait for something. Trust me. I know. I've only been waiting a couple of months and it feels like it has been practically forever." She was moving around the room, piling things on the bed as she spoke, pulling at me —then pushing me towards the bathroom, then on through to her room, nudging me into the chair next to her small desk, giving me no room to argue.

She picked up a long, narrow box and started removing things from it that I didn't recognize, using all manner of brushes to apply things to my face. She worked quickly, giving me direction every few minutes; telling me to close my eyes or to pucker my lips.

Exhausted and tired of arguing about the dinner and the party tonight—telling myself that I would slip away as quickly as possible later—I gave in and followed her prompting. Once she was satisfied with the results of whatever she'd done to my face, she went to work on my hair, brushing it out and then twisting it this way and that for the longest time.

Then it was time for me to put on my dress. She gave me no time to argue, gently pushing until I went back into my bedroom and tried on the dress.

Dinner was nothing like I was expecting—especially after my experience with the people who partied the afternoon away. The dining hall had been transformed into some sort of winter wonderland. Each table was adorned in a snowy white cloth, covered with an assortment of large and small silver dishes.

Hanging from the ceiling were silver decorations and long strings of thousands of tiny lights, large arrangements of white flowers and dangling curtains of some sort. The effect was nearly overwhelming, but it made for a very festive appearance.

The people were a surprise as well. Everyone was dressed in

what appeared to be their finest clothing, women in dresses much more extravagant than those that Eva and I were wearing and men in fancy clothes like I had never before seen... a sort of suit of clothing, with everything matching and looking like something that they could only wear for such a grand occasion. It made me wonder about the way the people here lived. No one looked or acted as if they were on the knife's edge of survival. No one acted as though they were in danger of missing a meal or going without clothing or any such thing.

How is it they can live so securely? They must have gone through the same event here as the people in the caves...

It made no sense. I knew, one way or another, I would have to get to the bottom of it, but Eva was pulling me toward one of the tables so I pushed the thought to the back of my mind for the moment.

This meal was very different than any other I had sat through here. There were no lines to form. . . in fact, the doors for the lines were closed off and practically everyone had found a seat at one of the tables. Instead, the covered dishes on each table contained the food everyone sitting at the table was going to eat.

At some unspoken signal, people began pulling lids off the

dishes and placing them onto small racks I hadn't noticed before that were stationed beside each table. When Eva pulled me to an empty seat, I saw that there were plates already laid out at each place. Once we had settled, she began to dig into the food that was being passed around our table. Again I followed her lead—though I once again took smaller portions than anyone else I saw.

The food itself was not a surprise, but it was the most delicious meal I had experienced yet. Everything was the perfect temperature, cooked to an exceptional consistency and the flavors exploded on my tongue. I tasted as many things as I could before my stomach began to argue with me. By then, people were beginning to get up from the tables and small groups were gathering and dancing to the music that was playing.

Eva rushed off to dance, pulling at me to join her, but I made a show of finishing the pastry I had just taken a bite out of and she shrugged as she went off to join the nearest group. I watched as they danced, noting that this at least was nice... calm... sweet almost—as opposed to the strange and erratic gyrating of this afternoon. Even when they started to form lines and dance as a group, kicking their heels up and spinning in a circle all together, it looked exceedingly different from that of this afternoon.

When they began making their way around the room, pulling people up from tables to join in I shook my head at Eva as she came close, but she ignored me and pulled me along with them. I was pulled toward the center as more people joined the lines and I did my best to follow along, clapping in time with everyone and attempting to make my feet do what those around me seemed to have no trouble with, even laughing at myself and a few others who were having the same difficulties.

When the lines started to break up, a young man took my hand and spun me around in a circle and then pulled me close, wrapping one arm around my back and curving his other hand around mine, guiding me with his steps and the pressure on my back.

I tried to ignore my discomfort, but being pressed so firmly to him was too much like the times I had snuck away to be close to Jude. I tried to pull away gently, but he only used the opportunity to spin me around and then pull me back against him, at which point I stopped being gentle. I pushed away from him—hard—and then turned to push my way through the other lines of people, weaving my way around other couples who were laughing and smiling and dancing.

I did not stop for anything. . . even to wipe the tears from my eyes as the pain in my chest exploded.

As I half-ran, half-stumbled in the shoes I was certain I would never become accustomed to, I ranted inwardly, consumed by anger. I wanted to scream, but held it back because I did not want to take the chance on having anyone stop me.

I had barely made it through the door before I collapsed in a heap of misery, the tears coming faster now, and accompanied by wracking sobs that shook me so hard, it felt as if I might just fall to pieces.

How long I stayed that way, I would never know. The time spun out indefinitely as the agony tore at me—and I felt as if I might break apart.

Sometime later, when I finally managed to get the sobs. . . and the tears under control, I pulled off my shoes before using the wall to push and pull myself into an upright position.

It took some doing to stand after that. My legs were weak and didn't want to hold me up—due in part to the ridiculous shoes and in part to the unfamiliar dancing. After a few moments, I made my way to my room, using the wall to hold myself up and propel my uncooperative body along.

Once in my room, I managed to get the dress off and then I collapsed on the bed, not even taking the time to pull the covers back. I lay there until my body forced me to move, sending me stumbling to the bathroom where I took care of my most immediate needs first. Turning towards the sink, I gasped in shock at the reflection in the mirror.

I didn't even bother to wash my hands. I just stepped into the shower, shedding the rest of my undergarments as I went. I cringed at the cold water that hit me first, leaning away and against the wall until the water began to heat up. Once it did, I stood under it for a long time letting the heat warm me, while the pressure of the spray began to ease the tension in my angry muscles.

After scrubbing my face vigorously, I washed my body, then stepped out reluctantly when the water began to cool.

I dried off, dressed hurriedly in my pajamas and crawled between the covers of the bed in a daze, dropping off into a deep sleep almost immediately.

THIRTEEN

Hope City

Year 45 A.E.

Day 176

The knock surprised me. It was still early. After the party that must have gone on for hours after I left last night, I would not have expected anyone to be up and about at such an hour. I was only awake and dressed because of the nightmare that had pulled me from my bed, unable to even close my eyes without the images appearing—to torture me again and again.

I wasted no time in moving to the door and opening it. It would not do to wake my roommate. . . especially since she would certainly be suffering the after-effects of the party.

But nothing could have prepared me for the sight that greeted me. Both hands flew up to cover the loud gasp that escaped before I realized I had even opened my mouth.

"Well, you're certainly all grown up." His voice broke on the last two words. . . and I was shocked to discover that I could see tears in his eyes. . . which I would never have expected. It was nearly as much a surprise as it was seeing him standing in my doorway.

A dozen emotions crashed in on me all at once, each fighting for space in my head—and my heart—but a strange combination of joy and relief and surprise won out as I threw myself into the arms of the man I had grieved over for ten years. . . the man I could never have expected to see again, much less here of all places. Choking out a word I had thought I would never use again, I cried, "Daddy!" My tears flowed unchecked as I wrapped both arms around his neck and held on for all I was worth.

"Oh! I've missed you, baby girl." His arms tightened around me, and somehow—in this small moment—everything was right in our little corner of the world.

How long we stood there like that, I would never know, but eventually the sound of a door opening somewhere made me realize that we were standing out in the open, the door wide open behind me—and I loosened my grip a little. "Should we?" I left the question open, tilting my head back toward the inside of the apartment as I asked.

He nodded and set me on my feet, though he did not let go completely, keeping one arm wrapped tightly around me as we moved inside. I closed the door as quietly as possible. I moved with him to the main living area, then to the wide sofa. I held tightly to his hand when we sat down, and I kept my eyes trained on him the whole time. . . for fear that I might wake up and find out that this was only a cruel dream.

We sat for what felt like a long time, me looking at him—and him looking at the floor, as if he wanted to speak, but had no idea where to start. When I couldn't take it anymore, I asked the question I didn't even know I had been wanting to ask. . . all this time.

"Why did you turn around? Why didn't you at least try to make it? Why did you just leave? Why did you leave me, Daddy?" And before I could even finish, the tears were there, flowing. . . fighting their way free. . . practically gushing, choking me while I tried to force the words out, my voice breaking on his name.

Immediately he folded me into his arms, one hand stroking my hair while the other held me tightly against him. "Oh, baby. You have no idea how much I wanted to get to you. I did try. I could have just set off without even trying to get to the gate, but when I saw him there, I knew I would never make it through." I leaned back. . . starting to interrupt, but he pushed on.

"It was for you that I did it. I knew if I tried to get to you, he would think there was a reason—and I didn't want you to ever have to deal with him interrogating you over what you did or didn't know. I couldn't have lived, knowing I put you in that position—so I left. I had to."

I could hear the reason in his words, but my heart refused to accept it. "You could have found another way."

He was shaking his head at me before I even finished. "Sweetheart, there was no other way." And when I started to protest again, he gently laid a finger over my lips. "You have to trust me. This was the only way to be sure you were protected, that your mother, my parents, even Orin—it was the only way to be sure that you were all safe."

"So, how did you know I was here?" I decided to ignore the subject for now, to pick it back up later when I had better arguments.

"I've been watching you, baby girl."

"Watching me?" I asked, not entirely certain I wanted to know the answer.

"Yes." He was nodding as he said it—and I wondered fleetingly if he knew what Sandy and her friends were up to. I opened my mouth to ask, but he went on. "I'm head of surveillance. I've been watching you for years—since just after I left."

"Are you serious?" Distracted from the thought of Sandy or her little stalker friends, I felt anger surge within me at the very thought. "Did you watch my friends being killed? Did you watch as the guard beat me and Jude and Malcolm nearly to death?" When he said nothing, I pushed on. "Why didn't you do something? Couldn't you see what was going on . . . with everyone? And you just sat here . . . doing nothing?"

"Eve, sweetheart, I'm not in charge here. They have rules—"

I broke in before he could go on. "You must be joking. That is the most pitiful excuse." I stood then, pacing away from him.

"They do, though. They have a lot of rules—almost as many as they do in the caves, and I can't break them." He spoke softly, adding a moment later when I turned around—so low I could barely make it out. "No matter how much I wanted to."

Looking at him sitting there. . . alive. . . I wanted to just forgive him, to tell him it didn't matter, to tell him it would be fine. . . I was here now and that was all that mattered. But the ice that had settled in my chest at the thought of my friends still there. . . in danger. . . the fear that something could happen to Jude—and I would never even know it—churned within me and the words just burst out of me.

"But you could break the rules in the caves. You could go off on your own and let us all think you were dead." I knew my raised voice would likely wake my new roommate, and I felt bad about that, but at this moment it was difficult to even care. "All these years, we've mourned. All these years, we've missed you. You could have found some way to let us know."

"And take a chance on that monster finding out, and using it against you. Or worse, using your lives against me? No. . . not a chance." He shook his head emphatically, but I pressed on.

"We could have kept the secret."

"No."

"Yes! I could have. I have kept your secrets all these years!" I wanted to scream at him now, to lash out with all the hurt that was surfacing. Knowing that he had watched me go through so much horror, thinking again of the friends I had lost and of the torture I had endured. . . all these years. . . while thinking that he was dead.

"Not a secret that big."

I turned away from him again, not bothering to argue with him anymore. He would have known that I'd joined the hunters and he had never once come for me. I paced the length of the room—back and forth—while the thoughts spun round in my head and the all-too familiar ache churned in my gut. *He could have easily gotten to me then.* The thought was a painful one. . . thinking that he had known and hadn't come for me was nearly as painful as the next thought.

But would I have met Jude if he had taken me away? Would Jude and I have cared for one another if he had pulled me out even just after I had started going out with the hunters? The thought was like a voice in my head, whispering to me words that I did not really want to hear at this moment, so I shoved the thought away.

It didn't really matter either way. I would never know. . . there was no way to know. But being separated from him now, with no way to get to him, to get him away from the caves, was such agony that I almost wished I hadn't ever met him. At least then I wouldn't have to miss him so.

"Eve, honey, stop. Please." He stood in front of me now, taking my hands in his to stop my pacing. "You and I both know that if I had revealed myself to you out there, you would have wanted to go back and tell your mother, your grandparents, your brother." His voice was filled with pain now—and I felt a twinge of regret for yelling. . . especially since I was beginning to see his point. It didn't help with the pain—or the loss, but it was beginning to make sense.

I would never put Jude in that kind of danger. And with that thought, I buried my head in his shoulder and let the tears come. They flowed through me, carrying with them all of the anger, the fear, the frustration, and the pain—giving me a whole new perspective on the last five years.

Suddenly I felt the weight of my own actions settle on me. I had unintentionally done the same thing my father had done. I had not been as close to the gate when I turned and ran the other direction, but if any of the class had been watching from the other side, it certainly would have looked that way to them.

Oh my. . . what did I. . . I. . . My thoughts were rushing around incoherently. I had turned and run into the forest, with no thought whatsoever about the class. They could have been right on the other side of the gate—watching. They all could have seen me.

Jude. . . what have I done?

Panic gripped me at the very thought and I could feel the strength in my legs draining. I sagged against my father.

"Eve, honey, what is it?"

I couldn't breathe to answer. Bright spots were flashing all over the sky in front of my eyes. . . there was tremendous pressure in my lungs. I couldn't suck in any air, no matter how hard I tried, and there was pain in my head. . . and my chest. . . and then, the whole room went dark just as I felt myself falling, tilting backward, heels over head and down. . . down. . . down. . . into nothing but a deep, black, dark abyss of nothingness.

The next thing I knew was an intense, stinging pain. I sat up with a shout and felt my hand hit something—hard. That pain momentarily distracted me from the stinging in the general vicinity of my nose and I concentrated on my breathing, trying to feel each breath as the air moved in. . . and out. . . of my lungs. . . as the skin and muscles of my chest moved and the darkness receded slowly.

The next thing I noticed was my roommate standing over my father with a long metal stick in her hands. "You know this guy, Eve?"

I couldn't help it—looking at her standing there in a thin shirt and pair of teeny, tiny shorts that no one would ever wear in the caves. . . holding that odd metal stick. . . looking as if she would happily break it over my father's head, all I could do to answer was laugh. . . and laugh. . . and laugh, until it was difficult to breathe again.

"He's. . . my. . . father." I gasped the words in between breaths and somewhere between "my" and "father", Eva dropped the stick and backed up, her hands over her mouth in obvious shock and embarrassment. She was shaking her head as she mumbled behind her hands. I managed to make out the words "sorry", "know" and something about a hanger.

At that, my dad laughed a little. "I don't think anybody made it all the way through the party without a hangover, Miss Eva. You're good," he said as she backed out of the room and then turned to run down the hall.

"What's a hangover?" I asked, completely distracted by the strange word and his obvious familiarity with it.

"Oh, my dear, there is so much you will learn over the next few months. I cannot begin to tell you how much you are going to discover and how much you are going to have to become accustomed to." He laughed, but went on before I could ask him what he meant. "A hangover is what you end up with the morning after you drink too much alcohol—and most everyone at that party last night drank entirely too much alcohol so they're likely all at least a little hungover."

"And here I was thinking Eva's joke about everyone having a headache this morning had to do with the volume of the music. . ."

"Which you didn't stay for, right?" He asked, looking at me with an expression that told me he already knew the answer.

"Yeah. . . because of my. . ." I looked away, not wanting to relive my experience from the night before.

"Concussion, right?"

I didn't correct him, only nodded a little, reminded that he had been watching me and grateful that he obviously had not seen my rushed exit from the party the evening before. He obviously knew all about how I had gotten here. . . *and likely everything since.*

I wanted to be angry, but it wasn't like there weren't people watching me all the time. Jude and I had known from the beginning that we would have to hide our relationship—because there were people watching in the caves all the time. Why had I expected it to be any different here?

"Hangovers and alcohol and parties like the one last night are just the tip of the iceberg, baby girl. If only you knew. . ." He shook his head and then moved over to pick up the metal stick Eva had discarded. "By the way, Eve. . . your new friend. . . you know who she is, right?"

"You mean Eva?" I asked, confused not just at the subject shift, but at the odd sound in his voice. Was he going to tell me she was dangerous or something? She had likely been trying to protect me when she'd come after him with her stick.

"Yes, Eva. She's the one the Chancellor pegged as the ringleader for that stunt a few months ago; the group of kids he sent out into the storm at two in the morning. . ." He looked at me as if he was waiting for me to catch up.

I sat there looking at him for several long seconds—waiting for his words to sink in. *Is he saying what I think he's saying?* I looked up at him—and he was nodding.

"You mean. . ." I gestured toward the bedrooms with a hand, limp with unexpected surprise. "She can't. . . I mean. . . You don't mean. . ." I shook my head a little, trying to dispel the last of the clouds that were still fogging my brain, moving my head sharply back and forth as his words began to make sense. "No, I don't believe that. She wouldn't."

He only shrugged in response—and then added a moment later, "I'm sure you're right. She's perfectly innocent. She was only going to brain me with a metal baseball bat a few moments ago."

"Baseball. . . bat. . ." I asked, but since he was already holding the long metal stick up as he spoke, gesturing toward the hall with it, I understood he was referring to it.

"Well, it's early and you're still dealing with your concussion—not to mention the after-effects of last night's party. . ."

I interrupted him quickly. "I didn't have any alcohol."

"Oh, I know. I meant all the loud music and the rich food you're not accustomed to."

I nodded, but otherwise said nothing.

"I'll see you at dinner?" It was obviously a question—and I realized that he was asking if I wanted him around, but also asking if I wanted anyone to know about our relationship. I could only nod—and then shrug in reply."

"Good. That's good. You get some rest then." He walked over to the chair where I was sitting and leaned in to place a quick, gentle kiss on the top of my head. "I love you, baby girl."

I smiled when his hand brushed through my hair a little, his fingers brushing down my cheek as he slowly pulled his hand away. "I love you too, Daddy."

Part of me wanted to ask him to stop. . . to stay. . . to talk with me some more, but I had so many things to think over, I wanted some time—needed some time—to do so, to figure out what it all meant.

FOURTEEN

Hope City

Year 45 A.E.

Day 176

I looked up at the sound of Eva's voice. "Is he gone, then?"

I could only nod in answer. She let a breath out in relief. "Whew, That's a relief. I'm not sure I could keep that up much longer."

I started to ask what she meant, when my father's words came back to me about the scores of children that were in the city, who the Chancellor had sent out in the cold, in the storms, over something *she had done*—not them—and I still could not believe it of her. She had been nothing but polite and flexible, despite everything, despite my lost love, my crying uncontrollably, my vomiting from both worry and from the after-effects of the concussion.

"I'm sorry. I had no idea who he was. I heard a loud noise and then I came in here and he was leaning over you—and you were just lying there." I nodded, but couldn't really think of anything to say—and she kept going. "I didn't know if he'd knocked you out or what. I just reacted."

"Eva, it's fine. . . really."

"But he's your. . ." She waved her hands at the door behind me —and I couldn't help laughing a little at the look on her face.

"Don't worry about it." I pushed myself off the wide seat and headed slowly toward the kitchen. "Honestly, I'm thrilled to know you're so handy. If I am ever being attacked, you're welcome to defend me with your. . . bat?" I looked at the metal tube she'd picked up and was holding loosely in one hand.

"Yeah. I didn't know what a baseball bat was either when I first got here. I actually got here just in time for the last of the games for the season. They start back up in a few months. You'll see then what it's all about." She set the bat against the wall and moved to the counter and started making coffee while I stood there in the doorway, staring off into space, floored at the thought of still being here in a few months.

Why her casual mention of it was such a shock, I had no idea, but somehow the idea of being here several months from now sent a wave of panic through me. Even though I knew I couldn't go back—I'd known that when I turned away from the gates—yet the idea panicked me now in a way that it hadn't before.

I turned and moved out of the doorway, leaning against the wall outside the kitchen, trying to calm my speeding heartbeats and the breaths that were coming in tight, little huffs.

"Eve, are you okay?" Eva's voice sounded far away, as if she were speaking through a long tunnel. . .

And then it was sharp again—and with it was the same pain in my nose from before—and I batted at whatever it was near my nose to cause such pain.

"Eve, it's all right. Stop." Eva took hold of my hand and stopped me from smacking the little tube out of her hand that she was trying to close. "Look, I don't know if it's just the shock of the day or your concussion, but you've got to calm down or you're going to end up in the infirmary."

She had hold of my arm and was pulling me, leading me back to the wide chair where my father had apparently laid me when I had fainted earlier. "Just sit here and relax. Don't think about anything stressful. Don't think about your father. Just breathe in and out and try to stay calm."

She let go and headed for the kitchen. "I'm going to bring you something to eat. You haven't had breakfast yet, have you?"

I had no idea if she was really expecting an answer, but I didn't really feel up to speaking and I was almost afraid to shake my head, for fear that the wretched nausea would return—or had already returned—so I just sat there, saying nothing. . . doing nothing.

A few minutes later she wrapped my hand around a warm mug and set a plate down in front of me. It held some of the pastries from breakfast the previous morning and was surprisingly appealing. Slowly, attempting to be over-cautious, I picked up the most plain thing on the plate and took a tiny bite, and then another until half of it was gone, and then I turned my attention to the coffee. Beside me, Eve let out a breath and pushed herself off the chair. "Good. You just keep doing what you're doing. I'll be right back." The next thing I heard was noise from the kitchen again, where I assumed she was fixing her own food and coffee.

By the time she sat down again—across from me this time—I had finished the first pastry and half of my coffee, and I was feeling much better than I had all morning.

"I tell you, I had no idea you were going to be such a handful when Astrid spoke to me about taking you on as a roommate."

I stopped, looking up at her in shock, but it took no more than a second to see that she was kidding.

"Relax, Eve. You're good. I've been there, remember. It's a lot to deal with." She waved away any concern I might have had and dug into her breakfast. A few seconds later, so did I and we ate in companionable silence for awhile before she said anything else.

"Listen, I've got to get ready for work. Are you going to be okay?"

I nodded before thinking—and when that mustered no negative reactions, I let out a sigh of relief. Of course, the relief was short-lived when I realized I had no idea what I was supposed to be doing or where I was supposed to report to. "What exactly am I supposed to do?"

Eva was already shaking her head. "Astrid told me you're not assigned to a duty station. You are ordered to rest for another day at least." When I started to argue, she stopped me with a hand on my shoulder. "Trust me, take the time. You'll work plenty hard. Enjoy having a little time to just be here."

She walked to the kitchen and set the plate and mug beside

the small sink. "If you're feeling up to it later, we can do a little tour of the city. It's really a great place." With a wink, she added, "when there are no crazy people partying all over, that is." And then she was gone, heading towards her bedroom.

I went back to my breakfast, still eating slowly. I hadn't finished when she came back through. "If you need anything, there's always people around. Just pop your head outside and ask someone." And then she was out the door—before I could say a word.

For nearly an hour, I found things to do around the apartment. I washed the dishes. I cleaned up my small room, putting away my dress, shoes, and underclothes from the night before. I would have to ask Eva soon about how we went about cleaning our clothes. . . but since the dress had no stains or areas where I had sweat in it, I didn't worry too much about it.

I went through the rest of the rooms, save Eva's, looking for anything that needed doing, but the entire apartment was in excellent shape so I pulled a book off the shelf and read for almost hour. When I realized that I had read the same paragraph five times, I knew I had to find something to do. . . so I put the book away and pulled on the thin jacket Eva had taken out of the box for me before heading out the door. It might not be as cold as I was used to in the caves, but I wasn't taking any chances.

Eva had said there were always people around, but I went all the way to the ground floor before I saw another person. It was a tall, slender man, who was clearly in a hurry to get somewhere. I watched as he walked by, glasses slipping down the front of his nose and his arms full of what looked like rolled up papers. I carefully sidestepped and then turned to watch him walk away towards the other side of the enormous room.

Since I had no specific destination in mind, I followed. When he ducked into one of the dimly lit corridors, I did too, careful to keep one hand on the wall beside me as I walked, but when I came to a junction, I realized the man was nowhere near enough to see. I turned right and followed along the wall until I came to another junction. Thinking for sure I would end up right back out in the open, I turned right again. I followed it until there was only a locked door in front of me, but the hall never led me back out into the area they called the stacks.

When I turned and went back the way I had come, I discovered that the floor was sloping upward. I realized I must have missed it before—when going down—because it was quite subtle. With my eyes beginning to adjust to the half-light, I could see the floor in front of me and the walls on either side, although never more than ten feet in front of me. The slope I had only noticed because of the extra effort it was taking to walk back up.

After a time, I began to feel a nervous tickle at the back of my neck. If I were in the caves, I would have been expecting to be attacked at any minute, but here in the city, it was supposed to be safer than the caves—albeit much more dimly lit. *Obviously the people who use these halls know them well enough to walk them in the dark.* I found myself wondering if there were better lit corridors anywhere. Since I had only seen the main area, the dining room, and the short hall leading there, I didn't exactly have much of a reference point.

And somehow, though Eva had mentioned taking a tour, I doubted this part of the city was intended to be toured much by those who weren't supposed to be here. *Although it isn't as if anyone has stopped me.*

Still, I worked backward in my mind, trying to remember precisely where I had turned, and did my best to reverse the directions in my head—breathing a sigh of relief when I finally did walk out into the light.

The relief was short-lived, when I realized that I was not in the stacks. I pushed through an unlocked door and found that I was standing in just as large an open area, but there were no people that I could see—and no apartments either. There was, however, a lot of light. . . and it was reflecting off nearly every surface as far as I could see.

The space in front of me was outside, though it was enclosed on all sides by walls, and the open roof was quite a few levels above where I stood, looking up. There was a covered walkway all the way around the outside made of stone and there were tall, rectangular stone boxes in a strange sort of pattern throughout the open area. The open area in the middle, as well as everything in that area, was covered or filled with snow, though not nearly as much as I would have expected. I imagined it could have been because of how far down we were —and that we were inside a building. It was also nowhere near as cold as I would have expected. Still, I pulled the jacket tighter around me, thankful now that I had thought to put it on before setting out.

I stepped further out and looked up. It was impossible to determine whether or not there had ever been a roof above this large, open area. It was too high to tell, but since the door had opened under a stone covering, and the main area looked as if everything was made of stone designed to survive outside, it was probably something that had been built with no roof.

"Do you like my garden, Miss Eve?"

I jumped. . . and screamed at the low voice that came from somewhere behind and to the side of me. As I turned to look for who had spoken—and where they were, I tried to calm my breathing. When the man I only knew as Alexander stepped out from under one of the covered walkways, I saw how I could have missed him. He was dressed in colors that were very similar to the stone all around us. He had likely been standing under and behind a stone—and he had blended right into his surroundings.

"Just how did you manage to find my little hideaway?" His voice was calm and even, but there was also a hardness to his tone that told me he wasn't happy that I had stumbled onto something he obviously worked hard to keeping hidden.

With nothing to hide. . . for the moment anyway. . . I answered truthfully. "Completely by accident, I assure you. I was looking around and I ended up at a locked door. I tried to retrace my steps, but. . ." I shrugged as I went on, completely unconcerned. "I suppose I took a wrong turn somewhere."

He walked out from under the overhang, moving slowly, walking past me, along the stone path that wound through the stone, maze-like area. "Well, that sounds like a natural enough accident."

He walked around behind me, talking as he moved—and I

stood completely still, determined not to give him any reason to think that he was making me nervous. "You are a very curious sort of person, aren't you, Eve."

When I didn't answer, he went on. "I've been watching you, you know. I know all about you, your family. . ." There was something in his voice when he said the word, something that made me wonder if he had been the reason I had been here several days before my father had revealed himself to me. "I know about your father. . . and I know about your boyfriend. What was his name. . ." He kept walking in a wide, slow circle around me, but I had long ago stopped watching him, looking straight across from me at the door that should lead back inside. . . "Oh yes, I remember now." He stopped in front of me, facing away from me, an odd expression on his face. "Jude. . . wasn't it?"

I felt the fingers of my right hand curl into a fist, but I held it behind me, keeping it out of sight. I forced the muscles in my face to relax, making my features show a look of disinterest. I was determined not to give anything away to this man.

"Alexander. . ." Astrid's voice drew his attention and I took the opportunity to take several deep, calming breaths and to relax my hands—both of them—as he turned towards her. "I'm sorry. I didn't know you were. . ." She started to back away, but he walked over to her. “What did you need, love?”

The sound of his voice threw me off. He might be good at playing people, but I couldn't believe he was so good that he could fake such a sound, the way his voice warmed when he said “love”, the way he walked over and took her hand in his. . . if he was faking either of those things, he was much better than I could ever have imagined.

It threw me off, thinking I could be reading him wrong.

Was it possible. . . that he really was just trying to do right by his people—and rescuing some others in the process? Could I have misjudged him? Watching him with Astrid, I had to admit it was possible, but I still wasn't ready to completely open up to him just yet.

I paced the room, back and forth, for nearly an hour before Eva showed up—and I was nearly in a panic. If he had given me some clue what he wanted from me, I might have felt better about the whole thing, but he hadn't.

He had walked back from Astrid's side, calmly and quietly escorted me out and through the halls into the main open area, barely saying a word the entire time. He hadn't even stayed around to speak to me. When I had turned to thank him, he had already been gone—leaving me no choice but to go up to the apartment. . . because I certainly was not about to go exploring on my own again.

"Eva, there you are!" I practically threw myself at her when she walked in the door. "Where have you been all this time?"

She stepped back a little and looked at me with a very odd expression indeed. "I've been working. Why?"

"Oh, you would not believe. . ." I stopped, looked at the clock and then back at her. "You've been at work this long? Seriously?" It was nearly time for dinner. That was a long day —especially given how early it had started.

She didn't answer though. She turned away and headed for the back of the apartment. "Do you mind? I have got to get out of these clothes." I followed as she headed to her bedroom, curious about what she wasn't telling me.

"Eva, is everything all right?" She didn't shut her bedroom door so I followed her in, half expecting her to tell me to leave, but too concerned over her strange behavior to leave it alone.

"Oh yeah. It's fine. It's just fine. Right as rain." She spoke sharply, each word hard as she stormed around her room picking up several items of clothing as she shed her outer layers.

"Did something happen at work?"

She stopped, the sock she'd been pulling on only halfway up her calf. "Nothing happened at work." She grit her teeth and then went back to pulling on the sock, speaking softly, more to herself than me, as she did. "Just the same old stuff." She pulled the other sock on, yanking on it so hard I feared she might rip the thing. "More people being rescued." She said this through gritted teeth—and I nearly missed the next thing she said. "Dispatches delivered. No big deal." She stopped then, stood and walked toward me, waving her hands in a shooing motion. "I need to change." And she shut the door in my face.

I walked to my room, completely bewildered by her behavior—and walked over to look at the clothes hanging in my closet. I wasn't sure if we were supposed to dress nice for dinner on a normal day, but judging by the clothes Eva was busily putting on, I figured it was a safe bet so I changed my clothes too, trying to choose pieces that were similar enough to hers.

When I heard her door open, I scrambled to finish getting dressed, picking up the boots and hurrying out into the hallway. . . not wanting her to go out the door before I got a chance to talk to her again.

“Wait, Eva, I want to talk to you.”

“I'm not in the mood to talk, Eve. Just let it go.” She didn't wait. She didn't stop. She just kept walking toward the door. And it was all I could do not to scream in frustration when the knock sounded. Eva was within reach of the door so she yanked it open and I fought against the harsh words that leapt to mind. . . especially when my father walked into the apartment.

“Miss Eva, good to see you again.” And he swept into one of the little half bows Jude had been fond of. Eva, on the other hand, blushed furiously. “It's nice to see you again, too. And may I just say again how sorry I am about this morning. I had no idea who you were. I would never have. . .”

Thankfully, he stopped her before she could go on. “I'm quite certain you would not; never fear. I am grateful to you for protecting my daughter so fiercely.” She only nodded, then took the opportunity to escape, cutting off any chance I had to find out what was going on with her.

My father turned to me, obviously unaware of any tension between the two of us. “Shall we go to dinner, dear?”

FIFTEEN

Hope City

Year 45 A.E.

Day 177

I bolted out of bed at the sound of a door closing, but Eva was gone before I could even get to my door. I rushed to the front of the apartment, but she was nowhere to be seen when I looked out into the hallway and I was not about to go after her in my pajamas so I stepped back inside and closed the door.

What could possibly be going on with her? The only answer I had come up with thus far was that she was afraid I would leave the apartment and move in with my father. While he had mentioned something to that effect, I liked living with Eva and would happily go on just the way things were as long as she wanted me for a roommate.

Of course, I can't tell her that if she never stays put long enough to talk to me.

A little squeak escaped me when a sharp knock sounded on the door I had yet to walk away from. I shook my head to try and dispel the thoughts that had started going round and round with worry, and moved to open the door.

"Good morning, sweetheart." Dad's bright and cheery voice was a bit overwhelming this early in the morning. . . and with such unexpected tension between me and Eva still, but I put a smile on my face and leaned in to return his hug. "Good morning, Dad."

He set me back on my feet and moved past me to the kitchen. It was then that I noticed the large package he was carrying. It was several boxes tied together, and he set them on the counter and started untying the string that bound them together. "Is that spunky roommate of yours up yet? Would she like to join us for some breakfast, do you think?" He held open the top box to show several delicious looking pastries stacked inside.

I shook my head, almost sorry to burst his bubble. He'd obviously planned for all three of us to eat what he had brought. "She's already left for work."

His smile didn't falter. "Well, that's early for her, isn't it?" He didn't wait for me to answer, which was good, since I had no idea of what to say. "Oh well, her loss." He looked at me with a somewhat mischievous expression on his face. "Bear claw, sweetie?"

I started to take one of the pastries, when the name stopped me. "It's not really a bear's claw, is it?"

He laughed delightedly. "No, it's not. It's just what they call it for some reason. Have one. They're great." And he took one for himself as I carefully selected one and looked it over to be certain it was not indeed the actual claw of a bear.

Once he took a bite of his, I did as well—and oh, but it was delicious. I ate the entire thing in a series of tiny, hasty bites and had actually started licking the sweet, sticky remains off my fingers when I noticed Dad was staring at me. "What?" I asked, with a laugh.

"You're just so grown up. I can hardly believe it."

I laughed at the ridiculousness of his words. I was sitting here, licking my fingers. *What about any of that could possibly make me look grown up?*

He kept watching me—and though I said nothing in response,

I was suddenly torn between annoyance that he had missed the last five years—and pleasure that he was here now, complimenting me. . . which probably influenced my comment more than a little. "That tends to happen in five years."

I was surprised when his only reaction was a nod.

There was a tense silence for several minutes while we both ate. Then, when he spoke, there was a change in his manner. . . even in his tone.

"Eve, there is another reason I came here this morning." I looked at him expectantly, waited for him to go on. "You will speak with Alexander today. He sent word to me that he wishes for me to accompany you."

Nerves took hold of me. The man made me very nervous—and after our last meeting, I was still uncertain of whether or not I trusted him. I had not been looking forward to this since he had mentioned it at our first meeting. I had hoped to find some information about the man, to prepare myself, to have some clue of what I was walking into, but there had been so much going on since I'd arrived, there had been no opportunity to do so.

I could ask my father—I knew I could. After all, he had been here for years—and his distrust of the Chancellor would have made him difficult to fool, but there was something in the way he sounded when he said Alexander's name. . . somehow I wasn't certain I could trust his opinion of the man.

"How long until we need to go?" I tried to keep my voice calm, but this was my father and it was obvious right off that I was not fooling him.

"Eve, if you would just give him a chance, he's really a good guy." He laughed and then added. "You never know. . . He just might surprise you."

"Who said I wasn't giving him a chance?" I worked hard to keep my voice loose, nonchalant, emotionless. I even added in a half shrug. . . but he still wasn't buying it.

"Eve, just promise me you'll try to keep an open mind."

"I will. I promise." I was surprised to find that I truly meant the words—even though I still felt he was untrustworthy, I also knew that if my dad felt strongly about it, there must be a good reason.

I told myself that I would give him the benefit of the doubt. . . until and unless he proved he didn't deserve it.

Several hours later, sitting in one of the overstuffed chairs in

Alexander's office, I struggled to hold onto that vow. I still didn't know how I felt about the man in front of me—even though my father had assured me he was trustworthy. I felt like I was literally stuck between a rock and a hard place. My father would expect me to talk to this man, tell him what I knew, share secrets and answer his questions honestly.

But I still had no idea whether he was working for the Chancellor or not. No one had shown me any sort of proof that would convince me one way or the other—and it wasn't like I could go and ask the man.

I also knew that if I didn't give him something, he would wonder why. . . he would assume that I was suspicious and I would never get to the bottom of it all.

And I will never have the chance to go outside again if he doesn't trust me. I'll never have even the slightest chance to find Jude and the others if I don't at least appear to cooperate.

Sandy and Eva had already as much as told me they wanted me on the hunting teams here. Whether this was all just a plot to uncover secrets or not, getting outside would be my only chance and I knew it.

I would just have to find a way to get on Alexander's good side.

So, I looked at my father and nodded—and then I turned to

the only man who stood between me and Jude. "What do you want to know?"

He questioned me for over an hour; asking about things I never would have even thought could have been secrets, about things I saw no reason to lie about, about the normal, everyday operations in the caves, things anyone would know. . . leaving me wondering if he really was searching for information or if he was just playing around with me. I answered each question, trying not to sound bored, watching my father, trying to gauge his reactions to the questions. . . and to my answers. There was absolutely no expression other than interest on his face.

And that was when he hit me with it—the curve ball—the one question I could never have seen coming. "Did you tell anyone in the caves about your suspicions. . . concerning your classmate Alan?"

I started to answer, but no words came out. . . not one. I stopped, took a deep breath and tried again, but I still couldn't seem to form a single word in answer. That was when I stopped trying to answer and thought over the question—and in thinking it over, I realized the answer I had been about to give was right, but it was also wrong. I hadn't spoken to anyone. But Jude had somehow shared the same suspicions I'd had. If I had just said no, I was sure he would have picked up on the uncertainty in my voice. "Not exactly, no. I never said anything to anyone about it, but. . ." I managed to stop myself before saying his name, still determined not to take any chances with Jude's safety. "some of the other students picked up on it themselves."

He only nodded. "That's all for now, I suppose. Though I may have more questions later." I nodded as he added, "I'll just pass them through your father. . . that seems like it would be the easiest way." I only nodded again.

He started to move towards his desk, obviously dismissing us —and something about the motion. . . his body language. . . filled me with frustration and I finally realized why I was having so much difficulty with trusting him. He had spies in the caves. . . people who were feeding him information. He had surveillance everywhere by the sound of it. He obviously had more resources. . . and he was just leaving the people in the caves to the mercy of the Chancellor.

And the question that had bothered me on some level since I had first met the man burst out of me. "Why don't you do something? Why don't you help them? Why don't you use the spies you have in place to help save more people in there?"

"Eve." My father put a hand on my arm, squeezed gently. "That's enough. You don't understand."

"Then explain it to me." I stood then, gesturing to the man who stood there at his desk, with his back to us, ignoring us. "Or let him."

"Eve, stop." He pulled me toward the door as Alexander turned around, his face hard, his jaw set, his expression unreadable. "Thank you for your time." Alexander nodded, but said nothing—and Dad pulled me out the door and along the hallway, shushing me when I tried to speak again.

I turned to my father as soon as we were out in the open again. "He knows what's going on in there. He obviously has spies who are feeding him all sorts of information. Why doesn't he do something?"

"It's not that simple, Eve."

I turned away from him with a huff. "Don't give me that, Dad. It is that easy. He finds a way to take in all of the people who are kicked out of the caves." I paced away. . . then back and again, while the words poured out of me in an angry rush. "And life here is so much more comfortable than it ever has been in there so they obviously have more resources here."

He stopped me then, turning me towards him. "Eve, listen to me. I know you mean well. I know you have the best intentions, but you don't understand. What you are proposing would mean war."

I started to interrupt, but he rushed on. "Whatever resources Alexander has are not the point. He has to think of what is best for the largest number of people. Do you think it's easy for him to rescue as many people as he has—without the Chancellor catching on, without him putting a stop to it? Alexander is trying to keep as many people as he can alive. War is never the way to do that."

"But what if. . ."

"No, Eve. Stop. Think. You don't know everything about him, but just for a moment think about what you do know about the Chancellor. Does he really strike you as the kind of person who would just give up his hold on the people in the caves? Does he strike you as a reasonable person? Do you think he cares how many people die under his unrelenting rule?"

I looked down at the ground then, shame filling my cheeks with heat. "No." He was right. I knew he was.

"Baby girl," He pulled me close then, wrapping both arms tightly around me. "You have such a good heart—and I can see that you want to help your friends, but Alexander has to think of all the people here. . . and all of the people there—not just a small handful of them."

SIXTEEN

Hope City

Year 45 A.E.

Day 177

I was grateful when Dad made the excuse that he had to get to work. I went to lunch, picked at my food, walked around aimlessly for what felt like forever—and finally turned to make my way back to my apartment—still with crazy thoughts swirling around in my head. . . but mostly disappointment, frustration, and anger.

It's all starting to make sense now, why Alan looked so angry when we found that secret city. He had been angry, but it had never been for the reason I had thought. He'd been angry because he knew the Chancellor would start taking us out one by one and he would never have enough time to get us all to safety.

Obviously, the Chancellor knew about the city. . . and he knew enough to know that there were still people somewhere near it. He'd obviously sent more than enough reconnaissance teams to check it out—so many that Alexander's people had been forced to mount surveillance everywhere. And it was obvious that a secret city was too big a thing for the Chancellor to let anyone in the wrong position know about it.

Adam might be the only one who was safe, because at least as a guard, he would have been deemed trustworthy. But whatever it was that made the guards trustworthy in the eyes of the Chancellor, Jordan hadn't managed to make it and Sophia would be alone without having the chance to even be bound to him officially. . . *so she can't even grieve properly.*

And what about the rest of them? Jude was still in there and he was obviously in danger. Sierra might be okay because she was on the hunter's team and some of them must know about it, but what about Lily. . . and Jake. . . could they be in danger? Sophia, too, but she would be in the hospital wing for who knows how long. Lily was much too impulsive to be an asset to them and Jake had no real reason to know about the city. He would be in botany soon and his rotations might take him outside occasionally, but most of his work would be in a lab. Surely he wouldn't be in danger, would he?

The sad fact was, they were all in danger. No one was really safe in there.

The sound of someone clearing their throat pulled me from my thoughts. I looked up and my heart stopped—it literally stopped. When it started again, I could barely believe what I was seeing.

The breath stuck in my throat and I wanted to pinch myself, certain that I must be imagining things. I had to be seeing things that weren't really there.

He couldn't be there. . . he just couldn't be.

It wasn't possible.

But then he said my name—and I was running, nearly tripping over my own feet, fighting the tears that rushed to cloud my vision as I threw myself at him. All I felt was the collision of our bodies. . . and then he was kissing me. I stopped thinking altogether—only feeling his lips on mine, his arms wrapped around me and his body pressed against mine.

The thought entered my mind that we shouldn't be doing this out in the open, but the relief was too strong, our connection too desperate, for me to care about what we should or should not be doing.

He was here. . . with me. . . and that was all that mattered at this moment.

I tried to control the urge to groan when he stopped kissing me, then his deep voice sounded in my ear. "Eve, where is your compartment?"

Fortunately, we were only a few steps from the apartment I would likely be kicked out of now. Eva would never put up with mine and Jude's relationship, that was for sure. "Behind you. Three doors down."

He turned, pulling me with him, keeping me so close, he was practically carrying me alongside him. When we arrived, I scanned my wrist to open the door, then we were kissing again before the door had closed. I vaguely heard it shut behind us, but with Jude kissing me and holding me tightly against him, it was difficult to concentrate on anything else.

How long we went on that way, I would likely never know, but the next thing I knew, Jude was backing away, then turning around, keeping me behind him.

And then the sound of Eva's voice, nothing like I had expected. "You must be Jude."

"I am. And you would be?" He spoke kindly, but with an edge

of suspicion, as if she had come to take me away from him.

"Eva, her roommate." Her tone was flat, emotionless, devoid of any spark or life at all—and while I wanted to shout my joy to every single person in the city, I also wanted to cry at the unfairness of it all, that she had lost her love—and now she would likely lose a roommate as well. "Welcome to Hope City."

"Eva, I'm sorry. We can. . ." But I didn't get to finish. She waved a hand as she opened the door and disappeared through it. "It's fine." were the last words I heard from her before the door shut behind her.

Jude turned back to me then. "Where were we, love?" And he was leaning in to kiss me again when a sharp knock sounded at the door and a sound not unlike a growl sounded in his throat. "They're going to have to come back" was all he said before he captured my lips with his again.

We both ignored the second knock. However, when the door opened a second later, I gasped. . . and then shrieked when I saw my father step into the room. I knew it would be obvious to him what we had just been doing—especially since I was still firmly wrapped around Jude—and Jude was leaning against me. . . while holding me tightly against him.

There was an expression in my father's eyes that I really didn't want to interpret—and I rushed to step between the two men when Jude backed up and turned to face my father, a territorial expression in his eyes.

"Daddy." I leaned back against Jude, trying to calm him. . . and myself. . . somehow.

"Eve." He stepped across the threshold, not waiting for an invitation. "And you would be Jude, I presume. . ." He left the words hanging—and left me wondering just how he knew about Jude.

"Yes, sir. It's a pleasure to meet you." Thankfully, he didn't miss a beat, reaching out a hand to shake my father's without a question, without showing a hint of surprise that my father was alive. . . when I had told him about watching him die.

Of course, this city has thrown everything we thought we knew right out the window, so that's not exactly a shock.

"Pleasure, huh. . . We'll see."

"Daddy." I hissed quietly—even though I knew, technically, he had every right to be a bit protective—given what Jude and I might have actually been doing right this minute, had it not been for his knocking at the door.

"Eve, why don't you go and. . ." He didn't finish, but I knew precisely what he meant when he looked me up and down, and

I fought the blush that rushed to my cheeks. "while Jude and I get acquainted." He said the words with an edge that told me I had every reason to worry.

"It's all right, love. I will be here when you return." Jude gave my hand a squeeze and then slowly let go of my hand. I looked at my father. "Be nice. I mean it." I left the words hanging there as I turned and rushed away.

When I skidded to a stop in the bathroom, the reflection that met my searching gaze was a bit of a shock, but it answered the question of why my father had reacted the way he had. I looked like Jude and I had been doing a lot more than just kissing. Two of my buttons were undone. My hair was a nest of tangles and knots. My face was flushed and pale at the same time, though I thought the paleness must be in reaction to Daddy's unexpected appearance.

I leaned back against the bathroom wall, feeling the cold of the metal coming through my shirt, and thought about what that knock had interrupted. What would Jude and I have done if Dad had decided to wait twenty minutes to knock at the door? How close had we been to doing what would have. . . in the caves. . . had us put outside the gates?

Taking several deep breaths, I straightened my clothes, splashed some cool water on my over-heated cheeks and walked back out of the bathroom, pausing in the middle of the hall, shocked at Jude's words.

"I love her, sir. I intend to bind myself to her just as soon as I am able." His words sent a shaft of heat into my chest.

He loves me!

The heat quickly turned to ice as I realized the seriousness of what we had almost done. I had gotten so caught up with my excitement at seeing him. . . kissing him. . . being held by him again. . . that I hadn't thought of anything but the emotions we were both caught up in. We were closer than we'd ever been to going so far that it might have been impossible to stop. . .

We had been dangerously close to doing something that would have bound us together in, if nothing else, punishment. Though I couldn't imagine the punishment being at all the same here as it would have been in the caves.

"Is that how she feels about it?" My father's question caught me by surprise. And I held my breath in anticipation of Jude's answer. *How does he think I feel about him?* How could he know how he felt about me?

"I believe it is." Jude sounded so much more confident about it than I felt.

"And if it isn't?" My father's voice was surprisingly hard when he spoke. "Don't you think you might be rushing things a bit?"

"No, I do not."

I leaned forward, trying to focus on Jude's words. His voice had gotten so low, I could barely make out anything. "I know precisely how fragile life is." His voice was filled with such sadness that I found myself wondering if he was speaking of his own father or if he could be referring to someone else. "I have seen firsthand how quickly we can lose those that we love." Pain shot through me at the sound in his tone that told me he was not talking about his father then.

My thoughts filled with questions. Who could he have been in love with that he had lost? Had it been someone who'd been thrown out of the city on that fateful morning? *Does he know she could still be alive? Has he put it together yet—that most everyone who was put out or locked out of the caves ended up here?* Panic suddenly rushed through my veins at the thought of Jude loving another girl.

If she is still alive. . . when he knows. . . who will he choose?

Who should he choose?

"I lost Eve once. I do not intend for it to happen again. . . ever." Those words. . . and the strength of conviction in his tone, should have been enough to calm my fears, but with what little connection we had—mostly physical up to this point—would it be enough if he was presented with both of us?

Where only moments before there had been joy, doubts now filled me, sending a paralyzing agony through my heart. What would I do if he chose someone else? I had already lost him once. . . could I live with losing him again—especially if he was here, where I could see him. . .

All at once, I was reminded of Eva, walking around with a hole in her heart, missing her lost love—and suddenly I had a new appreciation of how difficult it must be for her to watch her roommates pair up again and again.

When neither man said anything for nearly a minute, I walked as casually as I could into the room, struggling to keep my fears, my worries, my doubts in check.

Jude was the first to see me. He walked over and wrapped one arm around me, looking at my father with an expression I pretended not to understand.

"Eve, I guess I don't need to tell you about Jude having been rescued."

Jude's arm tightened around me a bit then—and I struggled to keep myself together. "I also came to tell you about your assignment."

That got my attention. I had been waiting for this—and though it paled by comparison to the news that Jude was here, it was good to have a distraction that might take my mind off losing him. . . if that was how it was destined to be.

"You've been assigned to hunting." I exhaled in relief while he went on, "I can't say I'm surprised—though I will still admonish you to be very careful. While the rules here are not so strict in some ways, they do still have a lot of them. Not to mention, you will still have the beasts outside to contend with."

A moment later, with a laugh, he added. "Although, you have proven that you're more than capable of taking care of yourself out there." I laughed in return, grateful that something had finally managed to break the tension in the room.

Caught up in the sudden excitement rushing through me, mostly at the excitement I felt at the chance to get out in the open, I started to ask him about Jude, but he beat me to it.

"I've been assigned to hunting as well, love." He held me so tightly, I nearly forgot my earlier worries. "What a team we will make, yes?" He was smiling so widely, I made myself nod and smile, but the coldness still had hold of my heart.

"Should we go to dinner, then?" When Dad spoke up, it was all I could do not to jump at his suggestion. Dinner would be the perfect way to put a little distance between Jude and me until I could figure out how to solve the problem of whether or not his past love had somehow survived and was here in the city as well.

"Eve, do you need to change?" I looked down at my more than slightly wrinkled clothes and I was sure he was referring to the evidence of what he had walked in on earlier. Heat rushed to my cheeks and I ducked out from under Jude's arm.

"How about if Jude and I give you some privacy. . . and meet you there?" He was already pulling Jude towards the door—without giving me much of a chance to argue—so I nodded.

Jude took a moment to walk over to me, wrap his arms tightly around me, and kiss me nearly senseless, before dropping me back on my feet and following my father out the door.

I stumbled to my room in a daze and likely took three times as long as it should have taken me to get ready.

SEVENTEEN

Hope City

Year 45 A.E.

Day 178

The next morning was the first time I felt as if I had finally found something familiar in the city. Jude knocked on my door at six o'clock for breakfast. He greeted me with a kiss that would have lasted longer, except my doubts pushed in and I stopped him with a gentle reminder that we didn't want to be late.

He nodded and kissed me again, pulling away with a little groan and a low growl, playfully nipping at my nose before taking my hand and pulling me out of the apartment. My heart ached at the thought of losing him. I wanted to say something, to tell him what I was concerned about, to ask him which one of us he would choose if he had the choice, but I was also terrified to ask because I really didn't want to know the answer, because I was afraid it wouldn't be me he would choose.

All the way to the dining hall, he held me close enough that we nearly tripped over each other's feet—and I let him. Every step felt like it was slowly killing me, but I was determined to have as many memories as I could to sustain me later. . . just in case.

Neither of us spoke. He held me tight against him, tucked under his arm as we walked, while others passed us in their rush to get there.

It was wonderful.

It was horrible.

He'll choose her—I just know he will. If she's alive. . . and here.

The entire way to the dining hall, it felt as though he was slowly digging the heart from my chest. Every smile was torture. Every squeeze was agony. By the time we stepped up to the line, I was ready to scream—and my head ached from holding in the tears.

Fortunately, there was an exceptionally large crowd and the noise level made it nearly impossible to talk once we had collected our trays. I picked at my food, hoping he would attribute it to nerves over going out of the city—and not pick up on my real concerns.

Following the directions to the hunter's section thankfully gave us little opportunity for conversation and my eating slowly had nearly made us late, so we had no time to duck into a dark corner on the way.

Once we arrived, we were swept up into different areas; me to the armory and he to wherever they kept traps and other gear he would need for what he was best at.

Once we were dressed, armed and laden with everything we would need for the day's hunting, we joined the large group of hunters who were lining up in the outside area that someone told me had once been a dock. I was grateful to get outside in the cold, decked out in all my heavy outer-gear.

At first, it took everything I had to not protest when we were told that Jude and I would be split up and paired with other hunters until we got the lay of the land, but I realized quickly enough the sense in that. We would need someone with us who could tell us where we could go and where we could not.

Jude did not take the news any better than I—a hard set to his jaw when he nodded sharply gave his feelings away—and, a few minutes later when we set out, he pulled me close, planted a quick, but intense kiss on me and told me to be careful, before rushing off to join his own group.

I turned to the young man whom I'd been told was responsible for knocking me out when I had been rescued. "So, you're a hunter, then?"

He answered with only a slight smirk. "Sometimes. I'm also one of the regular patrollers. That means I get to drag stupid cave-dwellers out of the cold when they end up too far from the gates to get back in time."

Recognizing an attempt to bait me, I did no more than smile at him as I answered. "As you say." And then, before he could think of something else clever to say, I added. "I'm not the one who had to knock out someone half my size. . . in the dark. . . on an icy lake. . . in unfamiliar territory."

"Yeah, but. . ." He shook his head. "Okay, you got me there. On the other hand, if you'd seen all the footage I have of the bad-ass hunter who stumbled where she didn't belong, you might not have been any more confident than I was that she wouldn't just shoot me."

"A fair point." I conceded with only a slight smile. "Shall we go?" And I gestured for him to go ahead—since he knew the terrain and I did not. He said nothing, just walked past me and out into the sea of white that was our world.

Several hours later, I had to concede that whoever had come up with this plan, had been really smart. Outside the caves, we had an immense forest and then mountains. There was very little area to get lost in, very few dangers other than the crazed animals who would not hesitate to kill us.

Outside the city was an entirely different story. Just finding a good vantage point to hunt from was a challenge. There were ravines so wide, I couldn't even see fully to the other side, a river that moved so swiftly it was only partially frozen, and mountains that I would never want to cross.

That was where things took a turn for the worse. Matteo had kept up a fairly non-stop stream of conversation since we had left the city, explaining that no one expected us to catch anything today—that it was meant to be an introductory outing only. I had started to ask about why we were so heavily armed, but it seemed obvious. They would still want us to have protection.

At a rise tall enough for him to show me a breathtaking view of the mountains that stretched as far as we could see and beyond, I made a comment about wanting to see their beauty up close someday—and he responded with something that shocked me so much that it took me nearly a minute to think up something to say in return.

"Oh yeah, they're beautiful all right. . . and treacherous in ways you can't even begin to imagine. Just pray you never get tagged for a re-supply mission. The weather gets better on the other side, but getting there. . ." He left the words hanging there and when I finally found my voice I asked, "Wait? Where do you go to re-supply? There's another settlement beyond the mountains? Somewhere with better weather? Why don't we all just go there permanently then?"

He didn't answer. When I looked over at him, his eyes were wide and full of fear. Clearly, he was not supposed to have told me all of that.

I was tempted to shake it off, pretend I hadn't heard anything—or that I'd misunderstood. . . something. . . anything. . . to find out more, but he was already scrambling back down the rise we'd come up to get here.

He didn't say a single word to me all the way back. He just fought his way through the deep snow and I hurried to keep up, while a thousand thoughts ran through my mind.

Is that what everyone around here is so keen on hiding? What sort of settlements are on the other side of those mountains? Why would they send re-supply missions across and not just evacuate everyone to a place with better weather?

And why do they not want anyone to know about them?

When we walked back to the dock area, I was not at all surprised to see my father waiting with everyone else. . . including Jude, who looked merely resigned. I could tell by the looks on both of their faces that they knew what I had discovered on the rise—the information Matteo wasn't supposed to reveal.

Anger exploded within me. *It's one thing for my father to know, but Jude knows, too! I have been here longer, yet they told Jude about all of this, but they didn't tell me!*

Seething, I didn't say a word to either of them. I just marched to the locker room, stripping off my gear as I went, passing my weapons to the attendant who stepped up almost as soon as I left the dock area, signing the digital screen he passed to me and then slamming the door to the women's locker room in my father's and Jude's faces.

I fumed the entire time I was changing. *Is there anything they haven't kept from me? Am I not trustworthy at all? What is the point of all this nonsense!* By the time I was finished changing, I felt ready to explode and I was seriously beginning to regret handing in all of my weapons.

The two of them stood right outside the door of the locker room, waiting for me, surrounding me the moment I pushed through the door. “Are you kidding me with this!” I stomped across the hall, but they both followed, not giving me an inch of spare room.

“Eve, if we could just get out of the hallway.” My father's voice was quiet. . . calm. . . infuriating. . . but I nodded sharply and walked into the empty room he ushered us both into across the hall.

Once inside, Jude took the opportunity to shed most of his outer gear—and a small part of me cheered the fact that he had been standing there all this time, probably sweating through all the layers in the much warmer air here in the city.

“Eve, what you have to understand is. . .” I didn't give him time to finish.

"You knew! You both knew! Why didn't you tell me?" I directed that comment to Jude. The sting of betrayal was much harsher than I could have expected, sharp and cold.

"Eve, I told you there were lots of rules here. This is one of them. No one is allowed to share information that is deemed classified without strict permission."

"Classified! Seriously, the information that there is another settlement out there—where the weather is better and people just might have an easier time surviving—that's not something you're allowed to tell me? Clearly, I'm the only one. How many other people are they hiding that from? Are you sure this Alexander guy isn't just as bad as the Chancellor—because from where I'm sitting, he looks about the same." I nearly spit the words at my father. The thought of my friends in the caves. . . the few who were left. . . the ones who would die soon if he had anything to say about it.

"Eve, we can't just do whatever we want. I explained this to you."

"No! You made excuses about it. You're just fine sitting here in comfort and luxury, doing nothing—as long as you don't have to see what goes on in there. You don't care at all about them!"

"I do care."

"You don't!"

"You don't understand, baby girl."

"Don't patronize me. I understand enough." I shot back, moving away from him as he advanced, trying to reach me.

"You only think you do."

"They're dying in there! We have to go now!"

"Why?"

His words stopped me short. Shocked, any further argument left me for the moment.

"Why? Are you really asking me why? How does that even make any sense right now?" I could hear my voice becoming ever more high-pitched, but shock and surprise prevented me from caring much.

"Yes, I'm asking you why. I'm asking why it matters because if this is all just some fleeting time—after which you and I. . . and all of your friends in the complex. . . are going to just go '*poof*', then why does it matter if they die now or they die later?"

"Well, it. . ." But words would not come. All the clever arguments that I had worked through in my mind while changing earlier fell flat—even in my own mind where they should have made the most sense.

I knew he couldn't honestly feel that it would be better to let my friends die. That was more like the Chancellor's thinking. *So he must be making a point of something. But what. . .*

"I must say, I am surprised that your grandmother hasn't managed to make a believer of you yet. She had your mother on board after only a month."

It hit me then. He was talking about Grandmother's faith. *All that praying. . . and look where it's gotten them.*

"Don't change the subject. I really don't see how faith is relevant here."

"I'm not changing the subject, Eve. This is the most important subject there is—and deep down you know it. And that is the problem, Eve. You don't see. You don't see where I'm going with this—and clearly you've been ignoring your mother and grandmother for years. You can't sacrifice some people for other people. Yes, we want to save them—all of them—and we are doing everything we can to make that happen, but we have to do it in the right way. . . and for the right reasons. That is what you don't understand."

"No, I do understand. What you are talking about is nothing more than an old superstition. It's probably part of the reason so many people died unnecessarily when that stupid moon hit, too. They were putting their trust in something that doesn't exist. The smart ones are the people who made it into the caves."

"You mean like the Chancellor?"

I nearly agreed. I had opened my mouth and my lips were actually shaped around the *yes* before I realized what I was about to agree with. "You are just twisting my words—trying to make it out like I'm the one not making any sense."

"Now Eve, you know that's not true. That's not what I'm doing."

I looked over at Jude, who was absolutely no help, standing there with a neutral expression on his face—and his arms crossed over his chest. I wanted to stomp my foot. . . or scream. . . because I knew my father was right. That wasn't him at all. He had always been the one talking straight to me when everyone else was spouting nonsense.

Maybe if I just agree to give it some thought, I can get him to go now. We can always argue this out more later—after everyone is safe.

"I see the wheels in that brain of yours turning. You're still not sold on the idea, but you're trying to figure out how you can get around it and talk me into going."

Again, the urge to scream in frustration burned in my throat. "Okay, yes. I'm trying to figure out how to get you to go. . . now. . . before it's too late."

I stomped into the apartment, past a stunned Eva, with my father and Jude hot on my heels, and slammed the door behind me—though I knew it would do little good. They would just follow. . . especially since Dad had found a way to get his code added to the scanner.

With a sound that was a half growl, half scream, I started yanking off my heavy clothes and throwing them into separate corners of my room. He'd known all along. He had known and he had told Jude. . . but neither of them had felt the need to share information with me.

And I am sick of it. I am over it. I am tired of being left out and told to keep secrets that don't need to be kept, of being placated and put in my place and then left out of the really important things over something stupid, some ridiculous misplaced sense of protection.

As far as I was concerned they could both go away. . . or just sit back and enjoy the stupid luxury of the city and forget all about the people in the caves. . . and then they wouldn't have to worry about everyone they'd left behind—and everyone who was still in danger. They could just go away and leave me alone. Both of them.

But I was not going to up. I was going to find a way to protect my friends, my family, the people who couldn't protect themselves, the people who would mostly end up here anyway —when the Chancellor decided they didn't belong in his city anymore. . . *at least, the ones he doesn't have killed first.*

And I am going to fight whoever stands in my way.

Somehow I will find a way.

. . . whatever it takes.

TURN THE PAGE
FOR EXCLUSIVE

BONUS

MATERIAL

DISCUSSION QUESTIONS

WARNING : SPOILERS AHEAD!

If your book club is reading ***Escape After E.L.E.*** and would like to chat or skype with me, please contact me via my website: http://jcmorrows.com/contact.

1) If you found yourself in a situation where you discovered that absolutely everything you had been told—by your family, by your mentors, by your leaders—was a lie, how would you deal with that. . . do you think? *Especially given that Eve has grown up thinking she is part of the last small pocket of humanity. . .*

2) Eve is quite resistant to any sort of faith in God. Do you think her experiences—and the lies she is now discovering—might be the reason for that? Why or why not?

3) The Bible tells us not to lie. However, Eve has just discovered that her father—who is trying to convince her of God's existence—has been lying to her and keeping things from her. Do you think his behavior will affect her continued resistance?

Would it yours?

4) Do you think Eve is correct in her mistrust of Alexander and the others in the city? Do you agree with her mistrust or feel that she should give them the benefit of the doubt?

5) Eve is more than a little shocked by the behavior of the city-dwellers. Do you think it is simply the bahvior or the marked difference in what she is seeing and what she grew up with that has her so shocked?

6) Were you surprised to discover that Eve's father is alive? Were you secretly hoping that he was all along. . . somehow?

7) In book one, Eve's relationship and lack of restraint has been critisized by some readers. Do you think it is believable that Eve would behave the way she does because of her lack of belief? Do you think she would behave in the same way if she had a strong faith in God and felt the Holy Spirit leading and guiding her?

8) Given Eve's attachment to Jude, and if his former love happens to still be alive somehow in the city, would you expect him to choose her. . . or stay with Eve? What do you think is the right thing in that situation?

THANK YOU!

Escape After E.L.E. is a book that I never actually expected to write. Book one in the series: ***Life After E.L.E.*** Was a story that I wrote completely on a whim—and I honestly never expected it to be published, so this book has definitely been a journey.

I could not have done any of this without the support of my amazing family. My mother and my amazing children encourage and inspire me daily and I could never live my dream without them!

And without my amazing readers and fans, I would never sell any books, so each and every one of you make this possible. HUGS!

And, of course, there is one without whom I would never have been able to do any of this; my Heavenly Father. HE knew what I could do before I was even born and HE has inspired and guided and blessed my writing. And He has blessed me with a miraculous circle of family and friends who see my talent, even when I don't —and encourage me to *just keep writing!*

God Bless you all!

~ JC

ABOUT THE AUTHOR

JC Morrows—best-selling author of Christian YA speculative fiction. . . drinker of coffee and avid reader—is a storyteller in the truest sense of the word.

She finished her first speculative fiction novel purely for the enjoyment of her mother—also known as her biggest fan, but of course she couldn't stop with just one.

JC has been telling stories in one form or another her entire life and once her mother convinced her to write them down. . . well, she couldn't stop.

But she gives God all of the glory for her talent and ability!

"And the LORD answered me, and said, Write the vision, and make it plain upon tables, that he may run that readeth it."

Habakkuk 2:2 KJV

NEWSLETTER SIGN-UP

Do Your Part. . .

If you have a personal blog, please consider featuring JC. If you enjoyed ***Escape After E.L.E.***, please consider rating this book and leaving a review on GoodReads and/or your favorite retail site. . .

it only takes a sentence or two. . .

Of course, if you love it and you're inclined to write more, feel free. . . and THANK YOU!

DON'T MISS JC'S BREATHTAKING ORDER OF THE MOONSTONE SERIES!

AND THE SHORT STORIES

OR THIS EXCITING NEW SERIES!

www.ingramcontent.com/pod-product-compliance
Lightning Source LLC
Chambersburg PA
CBHW010447310726
48979CB00018B/2846/J
* 9 7 8 1 9 4 8 7 3 3 4 3 4 *